THE BACK SETTLEMENT

THE Back Settlement

Margaret A. Westlie

Selkirk
STORIES

CHAPTER ONE

Beth Lord scrubbed at the worn wooden floor as if she were vanquishing an enemy. Always hungry, hungry, hungry. Her thoughts jabbed at her heart. Wanting, wanting wanting. I don't know why I am always so hungry. Her thoughts ran on despite her efforts to stop them. Be quiet. Don't complain. Don't need so much. Stuff the anger. Stuff the sadness. Don't cry. Disappear.

I wish I could run away, she thought. She paused in her labour and rummaged in her apron pocket for her hanky. She looked at the embroidery on the corner of it. Momma gave me this just before she died. It's the only thing I have of hers and I wouldn't have that if Poppa and sister Jessie had had their way. They sold off everything of value that was my mother's and what they couldn't sell, Jessie kept or Poppa burnt. The tears she had been trying to contain spilled over and ran down her cheeks. "Oh, Momma, I miss you," she whispered. She patted at the fresh flow of tears from her eyes. I wish I could just run away.

She entertained this idea as if it were new, but it had been with her for at least a year. If I could only just disappear and never come back, or stop living for just a little while. I'm so tired. She swabbed at her tears. It's no use thinking like this, I guess I'd better get supper started. She brushed back the dark brown hair that had escaped from its tidy bun and surveyed the contents of the pantry and found nothing in enough quantity to satisfy her father and brothers. It's leftovers tonight, like it or not, she thought. At least they'll be better than they were the first time round. Jessie never could cook a bird. And the pie, oh dear. She thought back to Sunday dinner and the look on Samuel's face when he bit into the cranberry tart. She laughed in spite of herself. "Serves you right," she said to herself. I've never seen anyone so greedy. I didn't leave the sugar out on purpose. She chuckled again. It was so sour even the pigs wouldn't eat it.

She continued to mull over the events on Sunday as she set the table. Poppa gave me a good scolding about waste not, want not. As if I didn't know better. I felt like a child. I guess I am only a child in spirit. At least that's what Jessie keeps telling me. How can she say that? It was me who kept things going around here when Momma died. She thought back over the last fifteen years.

She was so sick in the end, and the doctor couldn't find a cure. I was eighteen and seeing James. We were going to be married, but when Momma died, Poppa put an end to it. He said he needed me to keep house, but that's not all he wanted me for. She felt the bitterness and anger rise into her throat. Filthy old scut. James was shattered. He married Amanda soon afterward. Her thoughts were interrupted by the banging of the storm door on its hinges. Presently the kitchen resounded to the loud voices of her father and her brothers.

"Leftovers again?" her father said. "I told you a twenty-five pound turkey was too big for the few of us."

"It was Jessie's turkey," said Beth. "I had nothing to do with it." She closed her mouth firmly and began serving the hash.

"By the way, Walter stopped by this afternoon with a note from Caroline for you." Her father pushed aside his untidy grey beard and rummaged in his vest pocket for the crumpled note. He handed it to Beth. "And, no, you can't go, and that's that." He dug into the hash on his plate.

"You opened it!" said Beth. "You opened my letter!"

"There'll be no secrets in this house," he said around a mouthful of mashed potatoes and gravy. A dribble of gravy ran down his beard.

Beth swallowed hard against her anger and

her tears. She bent over her plate of the despised leftovers and found them as tasteless as her life.

She lay awake until nearly midnight reading her note over and over and wishing she could accept Caroline's invitation. She imagined a whole week with nothing to do except help Caroline with her new baby and visit. And the peace! A whole week of keeping herself to herself. The idea gleamed in her mind. Why shouldn't I go to stay with Caroline for a few days? I miss her so. She's more of a sister to me than Jessie ever was. I'm thirty-two years old. Why can't I go? Just because Poppa said I couldn't? She felt excitement rising in her chest. It's my chance to run away even if it is only for a week. I'll probably pay for it when I get back, but I don't care. She began to plan. I'd have to sneak out when Poppa and the boys are out in the barn. I couldn't take much with me, it's a long way to Charlottetown and I couldn't carry a heavy suitcase that far. Besides, I don't have very much.

She woke the next morning with the feeling of excitement still tickling in her stomach. She reviewed the plan that had come to her in the night. It'll work if I put on two layers of clothes and only carry a small bundle. That way they shouldn't notice. I can walk along the shore path instead of the main path. It'll be less direct, but I can do it. I'll cook some things ahead. That should satisfy them for a little while.

Two days later the pantry was well stocked, and Beth surveyed the results of her industry with satisfaction. That should keep them happy, at least for a day or two. She hastened upstairs to dress for her journey. She donned two dresses and two petticoats, stuffed her underwear in the pockets and pushed her toothbrush and comb into the sleeve of her sweater. There, that should do it, she thought. She modelled her bulky appearance in front of the wavery looking glass. Now if I can only get out of sight on the shore path before anyone sees me, I'll get away. She hurried downstairs, scribbled a note and left it on the table. Ten minutes later she was out of sight on the shore path. She looked back once but could only see the chimney through the trees and that only when the wind blew.

She strode along the shore path with a lightened heart. Soon she began to hum and then to sing. "Oh, ye'll tak' the high road and I'll tak' the low road, and I'll be in Scotland afore ye, an' me an' my true love will never meet again, on the bonny, bonny banks o' Loch Lomond." The song further lightened her mood, and she sang another.

In an hour and a half, she was halfway to Charlottetown and still singing.

She sat down to rest on a piece of red sandstone that stuck out of the earth just above the high tide line. This is a longer walk than I remember, she thought. The last time I walked it, I was only a wee *bairn*, and Momma carried me when I got tired. She thought back to her one and only trip to Charlottetown. It was such fun. Momma left the boys home with Poppa, and just the two of us went. We stopped and visited along the way so it didn't seem quite so long.

I wonder how Momma got Poppa to let her go to the city. I guess he wasn't as bad as he is now. Vague memories of the quarrels between her parents echoed in her mind. Maybe he didn't "let" her go. Maybe she just went. A cooler gust of wind made her skin crawl, and she shivered. She wondered at the cold. Maybe it's the memories, she thought.

She sat a moment longer then stood up and stretched and continued on her way. To her left, the water of the Northumberland Strait gleamed a steely grey in the afternoon light, what little light there was. Overhead, a seagull dipped and floated on the breeze watching for his supper. Far away over the strait, she could see the purple outline of Nova Scotia and New Brunswick. I wonder what it's like to live over there, she thought. I wonder if I'll ever go there. Probably not. I'd never have reason to leave the Island. The wind picked up, and she shivered. Nor money either. Another gust as the breeze became a wind. Beth pulled her cloak closer to her neck then slipped her hands back inside to keep them warm. She looked up at the scudding clouds that suddenly seemed darker than they had before. I wonder if we'll get rain out of this, she thought. Maybe even snow. She picked up her pace. Another hour of walking brought her to the ferry across the Hillsborough River.

The ferry was just ready to slip its moorings with a horse and a cart filled to overflowing with potatoes on board. Beth gave the ferryman her ten cents and perched on a barrel in the lee of the wheel house. It felt good to get out of the wind for a little while. Soon they were bumping and jostling their way into the berth on the other side. Beth jumped down from her barrel and wriggled past the horse and cart. "G'day sir," she said to the ferryman and was soon on her way up the muddy street to the general store.

She stepped into the store, and the wind slammed the door behind her. "I'm sorry," she said to the clerk, "the wind took it."

"Aye, 'tis windy alright." The clerk turned back to rearranging the dry goods according to colour and weight. "What can I do for you, miss?"

"D'you know Caroline MacDonald?"

"John MacDonald's wife?"

"Yes, that'd be her. D'you know where I might find her?"

"When you go out the door take a right, go up the street to the end and turn right, then take the first right and her house is the one with the two big horse chestnuts in the front garden. It's not far." The clerk stopped what he was doing and began pawing through the parcels of filled orders. "Since you're going that way, you might take this parcel to her. I had to order it for her last week, and it just came today. It's dress material so it's not heavy." He handed Beth the parcel. "She can pay for it the next time she's in."

Beth tucked the parcel under her arm, said good day to the clerk and was soon nearing the end of the street according to his directions. In ten minutes, she was rapping on Caroline's kitchen door.

"C'mon in, whoever you are," called Caroline from the interior of the house. "I'll be with you in a moment. Help yourself to the tea; I just put it down."

Beth stepped into Caroline's kitchen. Even though the day was gloomy and cold, the kitchen seemed to sparkle with Caroline's spirit. The tall windows were framed with yellow, dimity curtains. The white woodwork gleamed in the chilly light of the late afternoon. The floor was freshly sanded and swept. The kettle wheezed and sang to itself on the wood stove, and the full teapot on the back of the stove shone brightly from many polishings.

Beth pulled off her cloak and hung it on the coat hook behind the stove, then went to survey the contents of Caroline's pantry. Through the glass doors, she could see the heavy, white mugs with their cheery yellow flowers on the sides. It's just like Caroline to have everything matching, she thought. Her lips curved into a soft smile as she remembered how Caroline would always say: "Just because we don't have a lot of money doesn't mean we can't have things that match. It's all a matter of perspective. If you're buying dishes and your curtains are green, buy dishes that have a bit of green on them. It's good for the disposition."

Beth filled a mug from the shiny teapot and sat down at the table with its yellow tablecloth that matched the yellow in the curtains. It felt good to sit down after her long walk. She sipped at her tea and warmed her hands on the mug. Presently, she heard Caroline's footsteps on the stairs. She was singing a lullaby that changed to a delighted shriek when she saw Beth. The drowsy baby was startled awake and began to wail.

"Oops, sorry Catherine, I didn't mean to scare you. Beth, what in the world are you doing here?" She gathered Beth into a warm hug.

"You did invite me," said Beth.

"Yes, I did, but I wasn't expecting you so soon."

"The boys and Poppa were getting on my nerves so I thought: no time like the present."

"How are your brothers? Your Poppa too?"

Beth made a face. "Much the same only worse. At least, I'm minding it more. Jessie is her usual meddlesome self, of course. When they all get together, I try to stay out of the way."

"That bad, huh?" Caroline did a little rocking dance in the middle of the kitchen floor to quiet the baby.

Beth nodded. "Aye, that bad. The boys are rude, but Poppa is just plain cruel." She thrust the sudden remembrance of her father's last encounter with her into the recesses of her mind. His matted grey beard had made her gag, and he had smacked her for it. If she looked at her cheek in the mirror closely enough, she could still see the faint outline of his fingers—and it had been two days.

"You've put on a bit of weight?"

Beth chuckled. "Not really. I wore two sets of clothing so I wouldn't have to carry a suitcase."

"That bad." Caroline pursed her lips. "But you did get away without them seeing you?"

Beth sighed. "Aye, I did. I left them a note."

"Your Poppa must be savage by now. It's a wonder he didn't send one of the boys out after you." Caroline retrieved a mug from the pantry. She cradled the now sleeping baby in one arm while she poured tea for herself. "More tea?" She waved the pot in Beth's direction.

Beth held out her cup. "I expect they're only finding it about now. They were out back repairing fences." Beth chuckled. "The old bull broke out last week, and they had a hard time getting him back in. You should see the mess of Sandy's garden."

"It's a good thing it's late in the year."

"That's not the whole story." Beth took the teapot from Caroline and poured herself another cup. "The bull took to running and ran through the widow MacKenzie's washing on the line. He was draped with various unmentionables, and he ran almost to the smithy's before they could get him turned around."

"That must have been a sight." Caroline suppressed a laugh so as not to waken Catherine. She sat down in the rocker and began gently rocking and crooning to the baby.

"They couldn't get him into the barn. I watched awhile and then went out and had a talk with Bobby. He was my bull when he was a calf. I called him Bobby, and I've never thought of him any other way. We had a brief discussion while I pulled Mrs. MacKenzie's underwear off his horns; then I took him by an ear and he followed me into the barn as gentle as a lamb. Poppa said: 'I don't know how you do that' and stomped off across the yard."

"You could always talk to the animals," said Caroline. She shifted the baby to the other arm. "I should put you in your basket. I'll have you spoilt before you're a month old."

"Aye, but isn't it lovely to cuddle your own?" The longing was heavy in Beth's voice.

Caroline looked across at her friend. "D'you ever think of James?"

Beth glanced away from Caroline's inquisitive gaze. "I try not to. After all, it has been fifteen years, and he is a married man."

"Not anymore, he isn't."

"He's not?" Beth's heart leapt in her chest and she felt as if someone were squeezing the air from her lungs. "What happened?"

"She died this spring from the pneumonia. She went quick. She was a terrible lazy housekeeper. And James couldn't trust her to go to the store with a dollar for molasses but she'd spend it on herself and declare that the store was out of molasses. He finally started going himself just to keep control of the money."

Beth rose to refill her cup. The cold in her bones was finally giving way to the warmth of the tea and the companionship of her friend. "I didn't hear that. I just knew she was lazy." Beth sniffed.

"But that's old news. She was like that when she was in school. Don't you remember? She'd do somersaults rather than do any work."

Caroline rose and settled the baby in its basket. "I used to wonder how she ever got through school."

"I overheard the schoolmaster talking to Momma once. He admitted that he just passed her to get rid of her. Poor man! Momma was about the only one he ever talked to. She was as safe as the bank and minded her own business."

"She took a lot of information with her to the grave," said Caroline. She picked up her cup. "Are you warm enough now? I have to start supper, for John will be home and as hungry as a bear."

"It'll be nice to see John again. I haven't seen either of you since your wedding."

They sat up late talking and reminiscing. About midnight, they wandered up the steep stairs still laughing and trying to be quiet so as not to wake John. Beth tumbled into bed, pulled the blankets up to her chin and fell into a dreamless restorative sleep. She awoke at eight confused and disoriented as to her surroundings. Oh! I'm at Caroline's, she thought. She squinted at the clock. It's late. I'm always up at six with breakfast on the table. She stretched and snuggled into her blankets a moment longer, enjoying the coziness of their warmth. She luxuriated for a moment, then she got up, dressed and went downstairs.

"Good morning, you slug," teased Caroline. "I've been up for an hour."

"I am a slug, aren't I. I don't remember the last time I slept so late. I feel so good. It's wonderful to feel rested for a change." A frown whispered across her face, and the old fear knotted itself in her stomach again. It was the only night she would sleep well at Caroline's.

"You don't get a lot of rest at your house, do you?"

"No, there's always someone who wants something he could very well get for himself." Beth's mouth turned down at the corners. "I remember once Danny came and got me out of bed to go and get him a glass of milk."

"And he was how old?"

"He was in his teens."

"And I suppose you got up and fetched it."

"What else could I do?" Beth thought back to the event. "I knew he wouldn't leave me alone until I did, so it was as easy to do it first as last."

Caroline shook her head. "I don't know how you put up with it all these years."

"Believe me, I am hard pressed to do it day in day out and with not so much as a thank you. I've been wishing more and more that I could just run away."

"Why don't you?"

Beth shrugged. "Where would I go? How would I support myself?"

"You could go to work at the Charlottetown Hotel as a maid."

"They'd only come and fetch me."

"You could hire out as a lady's maid for some rich sea captain's wife. That way you'd at least have a half day off every week and some spending money."

"I could, couldn't I?" Beth's voice took on an excited lilt, then dropped again. "They wouldn't stop until they found me and made me come home again, and with Jessie living in town there'd be no escape."

"I guess you're stuck." Caroline checked Catherine's diaper and found it wet. She picked her up. "Come baby cat, it's time to change you."

"What are you going to put in your garden this year?" asked Beth. She leafed through a seed catalogue that had been in the magazine rack by the wood box.

"I haven't decided yet beyond the staples." Caroline spoke around a mouthful of safety pins. I can't make it too big for I won't be able to keep it." She fastened Catherine's diaper, then said more clearly, "I was thinking that I would try some of those zucchini squash. They look kind of interesting, though I don't know what I'd do with them."

Beth leafed through the catalogue. "Oh, here they are. Odd looking things aren't they."

"They look like cucumbers; that's what I thought they were at first. It says you can eat them raw or cook them. There's a pamphlet comes with them with a recipe in it for a cake. Though I don't know that I'd like a cake made of vegetables."

"It'd be worth the experiment to grow a few," said Beth.

The days passed much too swiftly for Beth and Caroline. Beth was grateful for a rest from her father's scowling demands and her brothers' temper tantrums. She cuddled Catherine as often as she could and wished with all her heart that she didn't have to go back home. Caroline was quick to observe her sagging spirits.

"You're not looking forward to going home are you?"

"No, I'm not. Not even a little bit." Tears filled her eyes. "I don't know how I'll do it after seeing you and John in your peaceful house with your beautiful baby." Several tears spilled over. She wiped at them with her handkerchief. "It's my home. I shouldn't dread it so much. But Poppa ..." Beth's voice trailed away.

Caroline looked at her with narrowed eyes. "I don't know why not. I would, given the circumstances." Caroline was rolling cookie dough. She brandished the rolling pin. "I'd whack them over the head if I were in your shoes."

The image of gentle Caroline whacking anyone with anything made Beth laugh. "No, you wouldn't."

"I'd like to." Caroline began cutting cookies. "It's a shame you gave in to them when your mother died."

"I try not to think of the 'might-have-beens.' In any case, I had little choice. It was that or run away with James. You know he wanted me to."

Caroline nodded. "I know. You told me that then." She grabbed a yellow potholder and wrenched open the oven door, then shoved the tray of cookies in to bake. "But wouldn't that have been better than the misery you're in now?"

Beth sighed. "Of course, it would have been. But I was brought up to obey, and I had never defied my father before."

"Unlike me." Caroline rolled out the next pan of cookies.

"Unlike you." Beth propped her chin in her hand and watched Caroline's deft movements. "I don't know where you got the courage to do that."

"I'm not as forbearing as you are, and when Poppa told me that I couldn't get married to John, that I was too young, I defied him and ran off with John anyway. When I stayed away overnight,

Poppa declared that I was 'defiled' and didn't speak to me for more than a year. Of course, I didn't mind that too much. What I minded most was being on the outs with Momma. Poppa forbade her seeing me."

"I remember how hard it was on your Momma." Beth pinched off a piece of cookie dough and popped it into her mouth. "I went to see her just after you left, and she was so sad. She told me to obey Poppa, that it was too hard on the family to do such a divisive thing as run away. I didn't think it would ever come to that, but Momma died soon after and Poppa laid the law down when I said that James and I were going to be married."

"I didn't know that you went to see Momma." Caroline tested the cookies for doneness, then pulled the first pan from the oven. They were thick and gingery the way that Beth's mother used to make them.

"She didn't tell you?" Beth tried to pick up a hot cookie and scorched her fingers. She dropped the cookie.

"You'd better let them cool a little." Caroline began greasing the pan for the second tray. "Momma never told me. She sneaked away a couple of times to see me. But Poppa caught her the last time, and she never came again."

"That's so sad." Beth continued to blow on

her burnt fingers. "Did you ever reconcile with your poppa?"

"When Momma died, he sent one of the boys to let me know, and that's all the contact he ever made with me. I don't know what he'll do now that we have Catherine. She's his first grandchild." Caroline fell silent. Then she said, "Would you elope now if you had a chance?"

Beth thought it over, then said, "If I had the right offer, I might."

"Is there anything I can do for you, Caroline?"

"You're getting restless, are you?" Caroline was mending one of John's socks, her lap piled high with mending to be done. "You could go to the store for me. I'll give you a list, and while you're there, you can give them the money I owe."

Beth felt her spirits lift. "It's a lovely day out there and not too cold, and I haven't been outside since I got here. A short excursion will be just the ticket."

"Hand me that paper, and I'll make a list for you. I don't need too much so the load won't be heavy." Caroline made her list then sat reviewing it. She tapped the pencil against her front teeth as she made a mental trip through her pantry. "I think that's all." She handed Beth the list. "Thanks. It'll save me a lot of steps. I find that having a new baby slows me down considerably. I usually get John to pick up what we need on his way home from work."

Beth pulled on her coat, warm and cozy from having hung behind the stove. She pulled on her mittens, then stuck the money that Caroline gave her inside the palm. She was soon on her way to the store. It was a brisk walk and just long enough to refresh her. She looked out over the harbour at the sun sparkling on the water and gleaming off the folded sails of the big ocean-going ships and the stubby smokestacks of the harbour tugs. The men loading them for their trip down the coast to the Boston States looked like June bugs from this distance. Beth stood for a moment watching until the chilly breeze reminded her that it was late autumn. She picked up her pace again and was soon climbing the few steps to the store.

"Good morning, sir," said Beth. The clerk was perched high on a ladder, dusting the top shelves with a feather duster.

"Good morning, miss, what can I get you this morning?" He climbed down from his roost in the rafters. "You found John MacDonald's, then?"

"Oh, aye, you gave me excellent directions. As a matter of fact, I'm running errands for Caroline this morning. She's kind of tied down with the new baby." She handed the clerk the list.

"They're doing well?" He scanned down the

items. "John dropped in a few days ago. He'll be needing new buttons on his shirt, he's that proud to be a Poppa."

"He is, isn't he. I've never seen a man take care of an infant before. They usually like to look but not touch, but John rocks her and talks to her, and she looks at him as if she understood every word."

The door to the store opened and then banged shut as the cold breeze caught it. Beth turned to see who had come in. She felt the blood drain from her face and her breath catch in her throat. "H-hello, James."

"Hello, Beth, I heard you were in town."

"I-I'm staying with Caroline for a few days. She just had a baby."

"It's their first, isn't it?"

"Yes, a little girl. She's a lovely child." Beth's breathing came back to normal by the force of her will. "They named her Catherine after Caroline's mother."

James turned to the clerk. "I need a fifty pound bag of flour and ..." James reeled off five other items.

Beth regarded him out the corner of her eye. You're better looking than you were, she thought, more mature and hardened. You've filled out nicely. That last thought made Beth blush and she ducked her head.

"Is there anything left on my bill?" James asked.

The clerk riffled through a pile of invoices on a spindle. "Just a piece of dress material and some candy that Amanda had charged."

James grimaced. "What does it come to, and I'll see if I can pay it now." He rummaged through his pockets for his money. "I've been going door to door to settle Amanda's debts. I'm just amazed at what she had bought, and I didn't know a thing about any of it."

"Oh, aye. My wife buys things without consulting me too, though I must say she has always kept me informed of her purchases."

Poor James, thought Beth, it's no wonder he looks so tired. Amanda didn't take care of the mending either. I can see where he has tried to grop up the hole in the elbow of his coat. She sighed. If you were my man, I'd take better care of you.

James turned back to Beth. "How're your father and brothers?"

"They're fine. They're probably still pretty angry with me. I expect I'll see them before too long, they must be nearly out of baking by now."

"Why would they be angry with you?" Concern rang in James' voice.

Beth made a slight grimace. "Because I was disobedient and left without telling them I was going. I just left them with lots of baking and a note to say where I was."

James frowned and shook his head. "You're not sixteen anymore either."

"According to them I am."

"Your order comes to one dollar and fifty cents," said the clerk.

James handed him the money. "Am I square with you now?"

"Exactly even."

James turned to Beth. "It was good seeing you again, Beth. Keep well." He turned and followed the clerk to the loading dock to get his flour.

Beth watched him go. The day seemed darker with his leaving.

Beth arrived back at Caroline's with her basket of goods. Caroline was on her last sock, her lap now empty of work. Beth hung her coat behind the stove and set the basket in the pantry. "You'll never guess who came in the store while I was there, Caroline."

"James?"

"How'd you guess that?"

"You're looking a little flushed and nervous, and that's the only person who could get that kind of reaction from you." Caroline's eyes sparkled with mischief. "Did you talk with him?"

"Briefly. He was settling Amanda's debts. It sounds as if there were a lot of them."

"Poor James. She led him a merry dance."

"By the look of his coat, she didn't take very good care of him." Beth's voice took on a disapproving tone.

"You'd take better care of him, wouldn't you?" said Caroline.

"If he was mine to take care of, I would."

CHAPTER TWO

I'm going to miss you," said Caroline. "You've been a wonderful help and such good company. I wish you lived closer."

Beth sighed. "I wish I did too. I'll probably be in for it when I get home."

Caroline picked up her knitting and began to knit with great concentration. Every once in awhile, she glanced at the grandmother clock on the mantle shelf. In awhile, there came a knock at the back door. "Get that for me, please, Beth."

Beth rose and went to answer the door. Her breath caught in her throat when she saw who it was. "James." Her voice came out in a squeak. She cleared her throat. "James, do come in. We were just having a cup of tea while supper cooks." Beth turned and led the way into the kitchen.

"Caroline, look ..." Caroline and the baby had vanished, knitting and all. "She must have had to change Catherine. Have a seat while I pour us some tea. Caroline will likely be back in a moment."

James took a seat at the table. "I'm returning to the Back Settlement this afternoon."

"I see," said Beth. She set his teacup in front of him.

"This'll be my last trip until spring." James poured his tea into the saucer, then blew on it to cool it.

Beth set a plate of molasses cookies on the table, then sat down at the other end and picked up her cup of tea. She sat holding it to warm her chilled hands. She stared down the table at James. "I see," she said again.

"Will you come with me?"

"I don't see how I can. It would be a disgrace if I went with you."

"Not if we got married this afternoon it wouldn't."

Beth opened her mouth and closed it, then opened it again. "I don't know what Poppa and the boys would say to that."

"Does that still matter so much?"

"No," said Beth. "No, it doesn't. It doesn't matter at all." She began to smile as the realization that it really didn't matter settled into her mind.

"So," James said. "Will you come with me?"

"Yes, yes, I will."

"We can stop by your Poppa's on our way and get your things."

"If he'll let me have them," said Beth. "He might be too angry with me to even let us in the house."

"It's that bad, is it?"

Beth nodded. "It's that bad." The memory of her father's liberties flashed through her mind, and she shivered.

James saw her shiver and frowned. "I can handle your Poppa and your brothers."

"Not all at once." Beth frowned. "In fact, you shouldn't have to handle them at all."

James shrugged his broad shoulders. "They'll likely be all bluster and no real threat. They always were."

"I don't want you to get into a fight with them. It wouldn't be worth it."

"Beth, I will be your husband, and of course it will be worth it. You're worth a great deal."

Beth ducked her head at the unexpected compliment. I don't remember being this shy with James before, she thought. Maybe because he never said things like that to me. She felt her shyness subside.

Caroline's footsteps sounded in the hall, and she crooned to Catherine quite audibly.

"I guess Caroline is giving fair warning of her return," said James.

"She's always singing to the baby."

Caroline stuck her head around the edge of

the hall door. "Ah, James, did you get what you came for?"

"I did, indeed."

"And are congratulations in order?"

Beth blushed and ducked her head again. "They are."

"So it's a good thing I invited Reverend MacLeod to tea. I see he's just arriving." Caroline laid a sleepy Catherine in her basket. "Come in, Mr. MacLeod, and welcome. We just made a fresh pot." Caroline's eyes sparkled with mischief. She took Mr. MacLeod's coat and hung it behind the stove.

The minister shook James' hand. "James Mac-Neil, I haven't seen you for ages. So you and Beth are ready to tie the knot?"

"We are," said James. "And as soon as possible."

"I don't suppose you brought your book with you?" Caroline poured him a cup of tea and set it on the table. She set out another plate of cookies for the men, then pulled up a chair to enjoy one too.

Mr. MacLeod felt his various pockets in search of the book. "I did, if I can find it. I never know when I'll have to perform a wedding." He began to dig in the bottom of his coat pocket. "Ah, here it is. I knew I had it. It's good that you are marrying." Mr. MacLeod tucked his last bite of cookie into his mouth. "It was a long time coming."

"Too long," said James.

"Let's, at least, go into the parlour," said Caroline. "It wouldn't be much of a ceremony in the middle of the kitchen." She rose and led the way into the parlour. She lifted a bouquet of autumn leaves out of a vase on top of the organ. "I picked these this morning. This is the best I can do for flowers. Every wedding needs flowers." She handed the bouquet to Beth. "There, with a little of that lovely colour in your cheeks and these red and orange maple leaves, you are quite beautiful."

Beth blushed an even deeper shade of red. "I think you two have been planning this."

Caroline laughed. "We three. Ever since the beginning when I sent you the note to come visit me."

"Matchmaker," said Beth, then smiled.

After the short ceremony of promises and admonitions, James and Beth said goodbye to Caroline and Mr. MacLeod. James gave his hand to Beth to help her onto the truck wagon. It was loaded high with supplies for the coming winter with only a small space left for James and Beth. "I guess you won't mind sitting close to me for awhile, eh?"

Beth could feel the shyness begin again. "I guess not." She forced the shyness into retreat. "I hope we'll sit close for a long time." She sat up very straight in her seat. "For years, I hope."

James clucked to the mare and flapped the reins against her rump and the wagon began to roll. "Goodbye," called Caroline.

"Goodbye." Beth felt a lump begin to gather in her throat. "Goodbye, and thanks." She is such a good friend, she thought.

It was a lovely autumn day. The sun was still giving a little warmth, and the air was cool but not cold. From the top of the street, they could see the wharves of old Charlottetown. They swarmed with men, tiny and silhouetted by the distance, carrying large bundles aboard ships with folded sails. Carts wended their way among the bustle on the dock, and sailors inspected the rigging. Above them, seagulls mewed and floated on the thermals ever watchful for a discarded scrap of food or a fish too near the surface. I just love this scene, Beth thought, then said:

"I wonder where all these ships go with all that freight?"

"Down to the Boston States, I would guess," replied James. "There will be a few that go north to Montreal on the St. Lawrence river too. Of course, they come back again loaded with supplies for here, and for Halifax and Pictou in Nova Scotia." He clucked at the horse again. "Come on, Tidy, we'll not be home before next week if you don't walk a little faster." Tidy picked up her pace, and they were soon at the ferry wharf. The barge that served as conveyance across the Hillsborough River was already half full, and James loaded the cart and the horse and tied her for the crossing.

On the other side of the river, they were soon on their way toward Vernon River. The company of travellers that had crossed the river with them gradually went different ways — some toward Bunbury, some to Southport, some, like them, toward Tea Hill and Pownal, and some to other small communities away from the main road. Soon they were travelling alone. The tree branches closed over their heads, and the woods grew silent as the birds and animals alerted one another to their passing. Bright leaves of red and yellow and orange rustled under the horse's feet and the wagon wheels. Brown oak leaves clung to their trees until spring.

As they drove ever closer to Beth's former home, Beth suppressed a shudder. "Are you cold, *mo graidh*?" James put his arm around Beth and pulled her closer to him.

It's lovely being called 'my darling,' thought Beth. She enjoyed the new old feeling of snuggling. "Not really. I'm just wondering what I'll say to Poppa. He'll be savage."

"Don't worry about that. I'll talk to him." He flapped the reins against Tidy's rump. She picked up her pace again briefly.

"What if he gets violent?" Beth shivered again at the memory of her father smashing dishes and kicking things and slamming doors when things didn't go his way. "Momma always sent me to my room when he got that angry, but since she died ..." Beth's voice trailed away.

"Why didn't you let me know?" James' arm tightened around Beth.

"How could I? He never struck me then, and he never struck Momma. And besides, you were married to someone else."

James sighed. "Aye, I was that." He was silent for a moment. "What are the boys like?"

"They learned their lesson well and were even better at terrorizing me than Poppa was. Remember that little cat I made a pet of?"

James nodded. "Sukey."

"I was busy doing something or other in the house when Danny wanted me to do something for him. I told him he'd have to wait, and he got instantly angry. Sukey was asleep in the rocking chair. It was her favourite place on a sunny day. Danny grabbed her by the neck and throttled the life out of her. I cried for two days."

"Are you telling me truthfully that no one ever hit you?"

"No one ever hit me then, but the uncertainty and the threat were there. It made life miserable.

Lately Poppa has become more violent. He struck me just the other day. He left a bruise. I don't know if you can still see it. After Sukey, I did as I was told and kept my unhappiness to myself. I almost went looking for you the day that Sukey died."

"Why didn't you?" James flapped the reins against Tidy's rump. She picked up her pace once again.

"If I couldn't have found you and they discovered that I had gone missing, there would have been the devil to pay when I got home. It was right after that you married Amanda."

"I see," said James. "I wish I had insisted that you come with me that last day." He cleared his throat. "I would have never left you there if I had realized."

"How could you have realized?" Beth thought back to the day fifteen years ago when she had last seen James. "We never told anyone. We were afraid to."

"Your Poppa is a pillar of the community."

It was Beth's turn to sigh. "Little do they know."

"Aye," said James, "he hides it well."

They travelled the next mile in silence. Beth drew warmth from James' embrace and marvelled at her changed circumstances. Momma would be happy for us, she thought. She always liked James. Beth smiled to herself then frowned. I hope Poppa and the boys behave themselves. She smiled a tiny smile. They won't like it that things have turned out this way. They don't think I'd have enough nerve to elope. Her smile faded, and the corners of her mouth turned down. Of course, if James hadn't come to get me, or if I'd said no, it would be a moot point.

"Penny for your thoughts," said James.

Beth chuckled. "You can have them for free. I was just thinking that if you hadn't asked me, or if I had said no, I'd be going back to face the music on my own. I just left them a note." She thought of the likely scene and shuddered. James pulled her closer.

"Don't think of what ifs," said James. "We're here now and married, and they cannot do a thing about it." He cleared his throat. "We're of age." He slapped the reins gently on Tidy's rump and clucked his tongue at her. "C'mon Tidy, we only have a few minutes of light left." Tidy picked up her pace again.

In an hour, they were turning in at Beth's gate. The light from the setting sun had faded completely, and the moon had not yet risen. The darkness was almost suffocating in its thickness. The faint glow of the oil lamp showed through the kitchen window.

"Whoa, Tidy." James pulled on the reins, and Tidy came to a stop in front of the kitchen door. Beth clambered down over the wagon wheel and waited while James tied the horse to the hitching ring on the side of the house. He turned and took Beth's hand. "Are you ready?"

Beth sighed. "As ready as I'll ever be. I just want this to be over." She lifted the door latch and swung the storm door open. The odour of burnt bacon wafted out into the night air. Beth made a face. "Phew! I wonder how many other dinners they've burned since I've been gone." She stepped into the kitchen and looked around. The mess of the once neat and shining room was evident even in the lamp light. She shook her head.

"So you decided to come home, did you?" said her father. The sarcasm was heavy in his voice. "I should take the switch to you, that's what I should do." His voice crescendoed to a bellow. "What do you mean by running away from here?" The air grew ugly as he began to curse at Beth. "You never were any good. Just like your mother. She was only good for one thing." He reached to grab Beth's arm. She jerked back and eluded him, bumping into James' solid frame behind her.

James stepped out of the shadows of the doorway. "Keep your hands off my wife. I will not have you speaking to her in that manner ever again." He drew himself up to his full height and flexed his shoulder muscles. He was no longer the obedient boy he had been. Beth's father began to sputter. Her brothers stood up with their father.

"What's the meaning of this? How dare you come into my house and tell me how to speak to my daughter. I'll speak to her any way I want to. Married indeed!"

"Go get your things, Beth," said James.

Beth scuttled past James and ran up the steep stairs to her loft bedroom. She grabbed the few possessions she called her own and stuffed them into a pillowcase, all the while listening to the sound of the men's voices in the kitchen below. At least there's no furniture being broken, she thought. I'd better hurry before this gets any worse. She hoisted the pillowcase over her shoulder and scrambled down the stairs. At least James is all in one piece and holding his own, she thought.

"Good riddance to bad rubbish," said her father and stomped outdoors slamming the kitchen door behind himself.

"Are you ready, then, *mo graidh*?" asked James.

Beth nodded and turned to leave.

Danny stepped in front of the door. "You do realize that you'll never be welcome here again."

Beth shrugged.

"Momma will be turning over in her grave," said Sammy.

"No, she won't. She wanted me to marry James. Now I have." She stepped around Danny and went out into the darkness closely followed by James. She threw the pillowcase on top of the supplies on the truck wagon, then climbed in over the wheel while James unhitched Tidy. He led Tidy in a large circle to get her turned toward the gate and home, then climbed into his seat beside Beth. He gathered the reins, clucked to the horse and they were away.

As they passed through the open gate at the end of the long lane, James put his arm around Beth. "There, now, *mo graidh*, my darling, that wasn't so bad was it?"

Beth held herself stiffly to quell the trembling in her limbs. "Not as bad as I'd imagined. What did Poppa say while I was upstairs?"

"Nothing you want to hear," said James.

"That bad, huh?"

James pressed his lips into an angry straight line and nodded. "Is that what you've put up with all these years?"

"And worse." Beth closed her mouth into a straight line too and said no more.

They travelled slowly in the darkness until the moon rose giving them its cold white light. Tidy sensed that home was on the horizon and picked up her pace. The shadow of a hunting owl moved over the empty fields. It dove. There was a squeak and a moment of scuffling, then the owl rose into the moonlight with his supper in his claws. Beth shivered.

"Are you cold, *mo graidh*?" asked James.

"A little." She nestled into the curve of James' body. He pulled her tightly into the crook of his arm.

"I'm sorry, I didn't think we'd be coming back so late at night, or I would have brought a blanket. But we're nearly home now. Just another mile or so."

Home, thought Beth. The idea of her own home warmed her, and she ceased shivering.

Beth woke early the next morning in the semi-darkness. The sun was just beginning to show above the horizon. The room was still night dark and shadowed. She blinked several times to bring what little she could see into focus. Outdoors a rooster crowed, then crowed again and the events of yesterday rushed into her awareness. James, she thought, then smiled. She slid her hand to his side of the bed. It was still warm. You haven't been up long, then, she thought. She lay there a moment longer, then got up, washed and dressed, hastening downstairs.

"You're awake. You could have slept in. Yesterday was a long day for you."

"I missed you," said Beth, then blushed.

"That's as it should be, *mo graidh*. You slept well?"

"Better than I have in a long time. Even at

Caroline's, I must have been afraid of Poppa and the boys showing up to take me back to the farm for I didn't sleep well even there."

"And now you don't have to worry anymore."

"It's a great relief." Beth took a deep breath then let it out in a sigh. "I must start breakfast. Porridge and eggs are on the menu. Will that please you?"

"It'll please me no end for I cannot make a decent pot of porridge."

As Beth fixed breakfast, the sun topped the horizon and filled the kitchen with golden light. In a few minutes, James came in with an armload of wood. The wood box was almost empty, and the wood rumbled to the bottom. "Do I have time to get another armload?"

Beth gave the porridge a stir. "I think you have. The porridge is almost ready, though it could stand a few more minutes of the fire. It won't be long."

Beth set the table and then stood in the centre of the kitchen taking in her surroundings. The walls were dusty with soot from many improperly set fires, the sun illuminated the streaks on the windows, the curtains were askew on their rods and dust bunnies hid out in the corners. The air was heavy with ancient odours of past meals and general uncleanliness. Beth made a face. I can see I've got my work cut out for me, she thought. She lifted the lid of the porridge pot and inspected the contents. She gave them a stir and moved the pot to the back of the stove to keep warm.

Beth surveyed the work she would do that morning. "Where might I find the broom and some cleaning rags?"

James shrugged into his jacket and pondered a moment. "I think the broom is out in the barn. I took it out there to sweep up some oats I spilled and set it in the corner of the granary. I haven't thought of it since."

"I can see that," said Beth. "The dust bunnies are breeding in every corner."

James put his arms around Beth. "It'll give you something to do with your day."

Beth stiffened in his embrace.

"What's wrong?"

She pulled away from James altogether. She hung her head.

"Is that what they used to say to you?"

Beth nodded. "Among other things and often." She swallowed hard to force back the tears and her memories.

"I'm sorry. I didn't know." James pulled her back into his embrace. "You don't have to do anything here if you don't want to. Goodness knows Amanda never did." He felt tears on Beth's cheek against his own. He tipped her chin up with his forefinger. "I didn't mean to make you cry." He rubbed at the tears with his calloused hand. "You can do as much or as little as you want; it won't matter a bit."

Beth sniffed back the tears. "I'm sorry. I know it won't, but the words were the same as Danny said to me just before I left for Caroline's."

"Is that all he said?"

Beth shook her head. "No. Those were not the worst. It was the name-calling and the ugly comparisons that really hurt the most."

"Did your Poppa never say anything to stop them?"

"Never, and after awhile he started saying things too."

"*Mo graidh*, I will never call you names or make you do things that you aren't ready to do." James hugged her tight. "I wish you had run away with me when your Momma died. None of this need have happened."

Beth hugged him back. "You couldn't have known. Neither could I."

James released her and gave her a kiss on the cheek. "I'll go get the broom, and you can use it or not as you wish."

By noontime, Beth had washed dishes and cleaned the interior of the few cupboards in the pantry.

She pulled down the curtains in the kitchen. These have been there awhile, she thought as she held them up to the light. Cobwebs hung from the hem, and the colour had faded so badly it was difficult to tell what it had been originally. I'd like to throw these out, but I don't know what I'll do until I can make new ones. She brushed at the streels of dust and sent a spider scampering for its life. I'd better ask James before I throw anything away. She folded the curtains and set them aside, then began to clean the windows. James returned at some point in her busy morning and stood the broom in the corner. He saw her industry and withdrew, closing the door quietly behind himself. Beth did not notice and came across the broom on one of her many trips to the back porch. James must've been here, she thought as she picked up the broom. The grandmother clock on the mantle clanked the hour, and Beth looked up in surprise. I didn't even notice there was a clock there. It's strange that I never heard it all morning.

The outside door slammed shut, and the sound of James' boots thumping onto the mat in the porch brought Beth to a real awareness of the time. I haven't even got dinner started. She began to scurry around, finding the makings of a meal here and there among the stores in the pantry. Thank goodness James had the foresight to bring home some canned goods. I'll have to bake this afternoon. I hope he thought to buy yeast so I can set bread. By the time I've made dinner, there'll only be a heel left.

She hustled out of the pantry with a plate of bread in one hand and two table settings in the other. "I'm sorry, James. I wasn't watching the time. I don't have any food ready." She set the table and scurried back into the pantry to get the pitcher of milk still warm from the cow. On her way past the stove, she pushed the kettle over the heat to boil for tea.

James sat in the rocker and watched her bustle about. He smiled at the sight of her busyness.

"You're laughing at me," said Beth.

"No, I'm smiling with pleasure." James continued to rock. "You are so unlike Amanda. She never cared whether I was fed or not. Half the time I had to make my own meals."

"Oh," said Beth. "I'd never do that to you."

James rose from the rocking chair and drew Beth into his arms. "I know you wouldn't *mo graidh*."

After Beth had washed the dishes, she rummaged in the pantry to find the flour, yeast and sugar for the bread. She saw evidence of a mouse in the flour bin and sifted the flour twice to make sure the droppings were gone. I must ask James for a mouse trap. Mr. Mouse cannot keep his residence in my flour bin, she thought. She proofed the yeast and melted the butter in warm water and soon had the bread dough ready for kneading. The work was strenuous but acquired a rhythm of its own as she rocked back and forth, pulling the dough forward and then folding it back on itself with the heels of her hands. Soon it took on the elasticity of well-kneaded bread, and she returned it to the bowl and covered it with a clean cloth. She set it in the warming oven to raise then went back to housecleaning.

Amanda was a worse housekeeper than anyone knew, she thought. She took the dust mop and dusted down the bead board walls of the pantry. Soot had even made its way in there and left streaks with every pass of the dry mop. Beth shook her head. I can see I'll have to scrub the walls too. I wonder where Amanda was when her mother was giving lessons, she thought. Her gaze wandered to the ceiling. Oh, dear, I'll have to scrub that too. She checked her bread and found it time to put it in the pans.

All week Beth cleaned and scrubbed and dusted. The musty smell in the air that she had noticed when she had first arrived lessened with each completed cleaning task. At last she had their home clean and fresh. She stood in the middle of the kitchen in much the same place from which she had first taken stock of her surroundings. The dust bunnies had been banished to breed in someone else's kitchen, and the windows sparkled as they caught the afternoon sun. The faded curtains had been cleaned and mended and rehung looking almost like new from the starch Beth had rinsed them in. Those will do nicely until next spring, she thought.

Outdoors the sun still held a little warmth, and Beth pulled her shawl around her shoulders and stepped outside. Trees sheltered the east side of the house and barns, and fields spread up and over the rise on the other side. The red island mud still carried the imprint of the last wagon wheel that had rolled across it. Ravens cawed from the darkness of the spruce trees, and from behind the barn issued sounds of chopping. Beth picked her way across the yard and found James hard at work splitting wood. His coat hung on a nearby fence post, and his shirtsleeves were rolled up to his elbows. His face was glistening with sweat and quite ruddy with the effort of swinging the axe.

"You're hard at it," said Beth.

James startled. "There you are, *mo graidh*." He pulled a red handkerchief from his back pocket and mopped at his streaming brow. "I was wondering when you would be coming out to see the rest of your new home."

"I have just finished cleaning, and it looked like such a pretty day that I couldn't stay inside." Beth bent to begin stacking wood in the wheelbarrow. "You shouldn't have to do this, James. If I'd known we needed wood, I could have chopped some."

"Was that one of your chores at home?"

Beth nodded. "All year. I did it summer and winter."

James frowned. "What was wrong with your brothers? Couldn't they chop wood?"

Beth made a face. "When Momma died, they decreed it to be my job and never so much as carried one stick again. Thank goodness wood is not difficult to carry."

"It's hard enough to chop." James picked up the axe and stood another log on end. "You shouldn't be doing this kind of work, Beth. Your brothers should be ashamed of themselves treating you the way they did." He gave the piece of wood a mighty whack with the axe splitting it from end to end with one blow. "You needn't do this kind of work here ever."

"That's a lovely idea, James, but I can at least fill the wood box from time to time."

James cleaved another piece of wood. "If you must."

Beth picked up the pieces of wood and filled the wheelbarrow to the brim. She tried to lift it but did not succeed. "I guess I filled it too full." She began picking wood from the wheelbarrow and cradling it in her arms. "Where do you want this?"

James looked up from his task. "Beth, for goodness sake, didn't I just tell you that you needn't do this kind of heavy work? Set that down and I'll take the wheelbarrow. I was going to stack it next to the porch door. That way we won't have to go far to get wood when the snow comes." He set down the axe and picked up the handles of the wheelbarrow. Together they walked across the rough yard to the porch door. "I find this corner is the best place. The snow doesn't drift in here quite so bad."

They stacked wood in silence. Soon the wheelbarrow was empty. "Climb in, and I'll give you a ride."

"Och, James, that's a silly idea."

"Have you never had a wheelbarrow ride?"

"No, the boys used to push each other around the yard in ours when they were little, but they never gave me a ride."

"Hop in, it's fun." James swept Beth up in his arms and deposited her in the wheelbarrow. He picked up the handles and soon was racing across the yard with Beth hanging on for dear life, squealing for him to be careful. He pulled to a stop by the pile of logs he'd been chopping and tipped the wheelbarrow so that Beth could climb out.

"There, now, wasn't that fun?" He grinned at Beth like a naughty schoolboy.

Beth straightened her skirts and smoothed back her hair. "Yes, I'll have to admit, it was just as much fun as I thought it would be when the boys were at it."

James picked up the axe and began splitting wood again. Beth filled the wheelbarrow to almost overflowing, and together, they stacked it alongside the porch. By the end of the afternoon, the pile of logs had been reduced to a few, and the stack by the door came up to the top of the railing on the porch steps. "One last ride?" said James.

"I have to put something on for supper," said Beth.

"Oh, c'mon, just one more."

Beth climbed in, and away they went around the barnyard. "Be careful, James."

The wheelbarrow struck a piece of sandstone and upset both of them onto the dusty dry grass of autumn.

"Having fun?" The voice held the hint of a chuckle.

"Oh!" said Beth and rolled onto her feet and shaking her skirts to a more modest height. "What you must be thinking!"

James scrambled to his feet, shook hands with the man and then introduced him to Beth. "You remember Robert?"

"I do." She searched his face for some clue to his identity. "Though I wouldn't have known you. It's been a long time."

"Too long," said Robert. He turned to James. "What do you mean by getting married again and never even asking your little brother to the wedding?"

James' brother, thought Beth. He was only about ten the last time I saw him.

"I didn't have time," said James. "I ran into Caroline one day when I was in town paying some of Amanda's debts and asked about Beth. Caroline filled me in and agreed to invite Beth to stay with her for a few days until I could get to see her. She did all the arranging, and we got married just before Beth was to return home."

"I hear it was a good thing too," said Robert. "The boys and Beth's poppa are livid. They were talking about coming over here and taking her back forcibly. They can't understand why she'd want to live away out here in the Back Settlement. Besides all that, no one in their family has ever eloped. It's a terrible disgrace so they say."

Beth rolled her eyes. "That's not strictly true. Great-grandma and Grandpa eloped, and they did just fine."

Robert laughed. "Of course, everyone but they would remember that."

"I understand it created quite a stir when they

came home. Momma told me the story when I was a little girl and swore me to secrecy, at least from Poppa and the boys. I forgot myself once and mentioned it to Poppa, and he just turned red in the face and stomped out."

"Well, he's more than red in the face now, I hear."

Beth made a face. "I expect he probably is. After all, he has to do his own housework and wash his own clothes, never mind cooking for himself and the boys. I expect it'll be fried eggs and mashed potatoes most of the time. He manages to burn everything else, and the boys are totally useless around the house."

"Not much use otherwise either, so I hear," said James.

"James! The boys are your family now too."

"Tell the truth and shame the devil," said James.

Robert laughed. "We didn't invite them to the *ceilidh* Friday evening. Are you two free or is it too early to ask?"

CHAPTER THREE

Beth sang to herself as she greased the tops of the three golden loaves of bread. They were fresh from the oven, their tops as round and perfect as Beth could hope for. She opened the pantry window and set the three loaves on the rack to cool. I'll take some of these with me to the *ceilidh* this evening, she thought, and maybe a little fresh butter. Her mouth watered as she thought of the coming feast. She swallowed and turned her thoughts in another direction. I wonder what James is up to today. I can hear him pounding out back, and he hasn't been in all morning. She put her coat on and went in search of James. She found him in the little barn.

It was the first time she had been in here, and she stood in the doorway a moment taking in her surroundings. The sweet smell of fresh sawn lumber was in the air. Tall windows along the wall behind the workbench allowed the outdoor light to fill the room. James was intent on his task, gluing and nailing, sanding and smoothing. He hummed to himself as he worked.

"Hello, husband," said Beth. "I've come calling."

James looked up from his job. "I didn't hear you come in."

"What are you building with such concentration?"

James applied another bead of glue and fitted the curved piece of wood to the object in front of him. "I was thinking that Robert's boy is old enough now for a big boy's sled so I'm making him one for Christmas." He began pounding nails to secure the runner he had just glued to the platform of the sled.

"It's a fine sled," said Beth.

"I'll have to take it to the smithy's to get iron runners put on it next week."

Beth ran her hand over the smooth wood.

"Careful, don't get a sliver in you. I haven't finished the rough edges yet, and it still has to be painted. I thought I could write his name on it."

"That's a nice idea. He'll like that." Beth watched James in silence for the next few minutes. "I must go and get dinner started."

James looked up from his work. "What's it to be this day?"

"I'm warming the rest of the rabbit stew from yesterday." She turned and stepped out into the cloudy November day. A flash of grey caught her eye as she turned toward the house. She searched her near surroundings for its source but could see nothing amiss.

I must be imagining things, she thought. She lit the candle that was in the space inside the porch door and went down into the cool dimness of the cellar to retrieve the pot of stew. The red clay of the cellar was moist to her touch as she carefully picked her way down the sandstone steps. A scuttling noise in the dark reaches of the cellar startled her, and she peered into the blackness but could see nothing. Must be mice, she thought. She carried the pot of stew upstairs and and set it on the stove to warm. She hung her coat on the hook behind the stove and entered the pantry to get the plates and cutlery. She looked at her two perfect loaves and was pleased with her morning's labours. She blinked and looked again. I made three loaves. I know I did. Where'd the other one go? That is indeed strange. There must be a tramp about, though they usually come to the door and ask. Ah, well, the poor creature must be hungry, living off the land as he does.

Darkness came early in November, and the air took on a cold freshness that it lacked at other times in the year. Beth and James set out on the walk to Robert's. James carried Beth's bread and butter in one hand and held Beth's hand with the other. In the sky, the stars sparkled in the velvet blackness of the night. Beth took a deep breath and held it for a moment before letting it go. There was a hint of the sea on the breeze. The moon rode low and orange on the horizon.

"It's lovely out tonight," she said.

"Aye, and so are you." James squeezed Beth's mittened hand. "You're not cold, are you?"

"No, just warm enough."

"You're not uneasy about meeting all the neighbours at once."

"I already know a few to see them."

"Of course," said James. "What am I thinking? You'd know them from communion Sunday, wouldn't you?"

Beth nodded. "And some of them would have come by to see Poppa on business. I never had anything to do with them so I can't say I know them. Poppa and the boys won't be there will they?"

"I doubt it. Robert has more sense than that."

They walked in silence for awhile. Farther on, the lights from Robert's house came into view, and soon they were knocking on the door and stepping into Robert's porch.

"Hello, hello, come in and welcome," said Robert. "Hang your coats behind the stove and find a seat. Johnny brought his fiddle, and we'll soon be having some music."

"Such lovely bread! Oh, and butter too," said

Elizabeth. She took the loaves from Beth and carried them into the pantry. "We'll be having a feast." Her round rosy face creased into a smile. "So you and James have finally tied the knot."

"And not before time either," said Robert. "I was worried you'd never get together, especially after James married Amanda."

Elizabeth firmed her lips. "Och, Robert, don't be talking of Amanda. She's dead and gone now and of no more consequence, poor thing."

Another knock came at the door, and Robert ushered in several more couples. "It's getting right cold out there," said Angus. He helped his Mary out of her coat and hung it behind the stove. "I was by the church today, and I see the horse trough needs patching. I'll have to get at that before snow flies." He shrugged out of his coat and hung it over the top of Mary's. "The work of the elders is never done."

The kitchen and dining room were soon filled with friends and neighbours. The news was passed and speculations were made. There was much laughter and teasing. Beth sat with the other women and let the talk ebb and flow around her. Snatches of conversation caught her attention and then flowed on.

"… missing a whole plate," said Mary.

"Not you, too," said Janet MacLeod. "There was a whole quarter round of cheese gone from the dairy, and I can't seem to keep the cats in milk lately."

Beth frowned. "I lost a whole loaf of bread today, too. I thought it must be a tramp. I know they're around this time of year."

"If there's one around, he's not moving on very fast. I've been missing a little of this and a little of that for three weeks now," said Maggie Moore.

"It's funny no one has seen him," said Mattie. "They usually come to the door when they want a handout."

The sound of the fiddle being tuned took their attention, and soon everyone was calling out the names of tunes and tapping their feet in time to the notes. Someone asked for a couple of big spoons, and there was soon a rhythm section as well. Murdoch Moore jumped up and did a step dance.

"Aye, Murdoch, you're a fine dancer," said Johnny.

"And you're a fine fiddler."

"Let's have another." Someone called out a tune, and Johnny tested the tune of his instrument and was soon away into another tune of his ancestors.

"Play 'Skye Boat Song'," said James.

The sad sweet song of Bonny Prince Charlie from long ago filled the rooms. Beth started to hum.

"Sing us a tune, then, Beth," said Elizabeth.

"Och, I can't sing, only to myself," said Beth.

"C'mon now, don't be shy."

Beth cleared her throat and slipped into the strains of "Annie Laurie."

"Oh, that was lovely," said Mary. "Sing us another."

Beth sat up straight and sang "Loch Lomond." "There now, that's enough out of me," she said when she had finished.

"It was lovely altogether," said Johnny.

"I need some help in the pantry," said Elizabeth. She pushed the kettle over the stove to make tea. "A couple of you men can pull the table away from the wall so we can walk around it."

Beth rose and made her way to the pantry. "Where do you keep your bread knife?" she asked Elizabeth.

"Top drawer, right hand side." She began passing plates and bowls to the ladies setting up the feast. In a few minutes, the table was laden with the abundance of summer gardens: creamy potato salad, yellow cheese, sliced beef and sliced ham, crusty bread fresh from the oven that day, golden butter stamped with the donor's own mark, rosy jams and jellies, and cakes and pies. It was a feast for the eyes as well as the palate.

Soon the only sound in the kitchen was the clink of knives and forks and the murmurs of appreciation. Elizabeth swallowed the last bite, set her plate down and said: "I have an announcement to make." The murmuring and clattering ceased. "Since this is the first time we've all been together since Beth and James got married, I want to offer congratulations from us all and to gift them with this that we have all contributed to." She pulled a package wrapped in brown paper from behind the stove. It was tied with lengths of brightly coloured yarn, red and yellow and green. She handed the package to Beth.

"Oh, my," said Beth. "I certainly wasn't expecting a surprise." She took the package from Elizabeth and held it in her hands.

"That's why it's called a surprise," said Elizabeth. "Now, for goodness sake, open it."

Beth pulled at the strings, and the package came open. It was a set of nesting bowls glazed in brown and with a pattern of flowers imprinted in the band around the top. "Oh," said Beth, "they're just lovely." Her eyes filled with tears. She blinked them away. "These are just what I need. I had to set the bread in the stew pot to let it rise this morning. Thank you all. This means so much to me."

"And to me too," said James. He squeezed Beth's hand. "I know I can expect some fine baking out of these. Many thanks."

"Well, now, finish up everyone, and we'll have another tune," said Elizabeth. The scraping of plates began again, and the conversations ebbed and flowed around Beth and James. Beth's heart was filled to overflowing with the generosity and kindness of her neighbours.

After the meal, there were a few more tunes and a dance or two, and then Johnny played "Auld Lang Syne."

"I guess that's our cue that the party's over," said Murdoch.

"I cannot play another note," said Johnny. He loosened his bow and set the fiddle in its case just as the grandmother clock on the mantle shelf began to chime midnight.

"It has been a grand *ceilidh*," said James. He helped Beth into her coat.

"Thank you so much," said Beth. "It was lovely, indeed."

"Don't you be a stranger, now," said Elizabeth. "We're not that far away."

"I won't," said Beth.

They filed out as a group and walked with the crowd, families dropping off at their own gates until only Beth and James were left. They walked on in companionable silence. Then James said, "So you had a good time."

"Oh, yes," said Beth. "I felt very welcome, as if I belong here."

"You do," said James. "These are your people now."

§

Over the next few weeks, Beth and James made their house snug for the winter. James banked the house and put on the storm doors and storm windows. Beth helped. She made biscuits and cakes in her new bowls. As was becoming her habit, she set things in the pantry window to cool until the weather became too cold to leave the window open for long. Always, there were fewer biscuits, and once a whole chunk of the cake she had baked for the Sabbath was gone.

"James, did you take a piece of the cake that I made this afternoon?"

Just in from the barn, James pulled off his coat and hung it behind the stove. "I didn't even know that you'd made a cake."

"I don't think we have mice big enough to eat the whole corner." She showed the cake with its missing piece to James.

"That is a puzzle," said James.

"D'you suppose we have tramps?"

James thought a moment. "They usually come to the door." He settled into the rocking chair and propped his stockinged feet on the open oven door. "Maybe it's a raven. They can be terrible thieves, and they'll eat almost anything."

"I think I'll set a trap for him, whoever he is."

That afternoon, Beth put the cake back in the window and left the window open wide enough to accommodate a hand or a beak. "You keep an eye on this from the barn, James, and if we're lucky, we'll catch the thief."

"I'll keep as much of an eye as I can," said James. "I'm just making the barn snug for the winter so I may not see anything."

"I'll be watching from in here too," said Beth. She pulled a chair closer to the stove and in line with the pantry window and took up her knitting. James kissed her and went out of the door, pulling his coat on as he went. Beth knit in silence for quite some time. Then the flash of grey that she'd seen before caught her attention. She rose from her chair and hastened to the pantry window to see a dirty hand reaching in to help itself to another piece of cake. Beth grabbed the hand and held on until the boy bit her hard enough to leave marks. She let go, and a boy about nine years old began running across the yard to the woodlot behind the barn. James looked up from his work as the boy appeared around the side of the barn. The boy went to scale the fence, and James caught him by the ankle so that he fell back into the barnyard. He began to squall and fight to no avail. James had him firmly around his middle, facing away from him so that the boy couldn't kick to advantage. He carried him into the house and shut the door behind himself before he released him.

"See what I found," said James. "He's a grand fighter despite his size. He landed a few good kicks until I could get my shins out of harm's way."

"Aye," said Beth, "he's a grand biter too. He drew blood when he bit me."

"What's your name, son?" asked James.

The boy stared at the floor.

"C'mon, now, we won't hurt you,"said Beth. She took in the boy's dishevelled, dirty coat and ragged trousers. A stench of unwashed body rose from his person as he warmed in the heat of the stove. "Whoever you belong to isn't taking very good care of you."

The boy continued to stare at the floor, saying nothing.

"You've been helping yourself to our food and accommodations for several weeks now. The least you can do is say thank you."

The boy looked up. "Thank you." His gaze returned to the floor.

"If we're going to help you, you'll have to tell us your name," said Beth.

"'Tis Roddy."

"Where are you from, Roddy?"

"Clyde River." Roddy continued to gaze at the floor.

"Why are you here?" asked James.

"No place else to go."

"Come now," said Beth, "you must have some family."

"Not anymore. Poppa threw me out."

"At your age? That seems unlikely."

Roddy shrugged. "He didn't quite throw me out. He just hit me and cussed at me once too often, and I left."

"Won't your family miss you?" asked Beth.

"Naw, there's thirteen more of us and not enough food to go around."

"Don't you miss your family?"

"Sometimes."

James and Beth exchanged glances. "What are we going to do with him?"

Beth looked across at Roddy and sniffed. "We have plenty. We could let him stay here."

"Can you work?" asked James.

"I can do most anything," said Roddy.

"Will you work?" asked Beth.

"Aye," said Roddy, "but only if you don't cuss at me."

"We don't use those sorts of words in this house," said James.

"We'll have to get you some clean clothes," said Beth.

"Ones that fit," said James.

"And a bath." Beth wrinkled her nose at the increasing stench of unwashed boy.

"I think there's a pair of pants and a shirt

upstairs that might fit him," said James. "They belonged to Robert's oldest. He had them on the day he went to see the piglets." James chuckled. "He was trying to climb the fence into the pigpen to pick one up, and he fell in at the dirty end."

"Oh, my," said Beth, "he must have been a sight."

"A smell too," said James. "He hasn't lived that one down yet."

James attended to the cleansing of Roddy while Beth went to find the clothes. She could hear their voices coming from the kitchen. "Scrub that too," James said. "And behind those ears. Inside too."

"Momma never made me wash this much," said Roddy.

"With fourteen children, I doubt she had enough time to do more than dip and dry."

Beth rejoined them in the kitchen just as James was wrapping the towel around Roddy and helping him out of the tub. "You're quite handsome underneath all the dirt. How long has it been since you had a bath?"

"About since Christmastime."

Beth rolled her eyes and shook her head. "That'll never do around here. Once a week, at least, with a mop up in between." Beth handed James the trousers and shirt, a pair of James' socks, and a sweater that looked like it had been shrunk in the wash. "This'll do until I can sew some other clothes for him. And now I must put supper on."

The rich odour of beef roast filled the kitchen over-laid with the fragrance of baking biscuits. Roddy sat on the lounge and watched.

"What are you so fascinated with?" asked James.

"She's so pretty, and she doesn't clatter like Momma always did." He swallowed the saliva that was threatening to overrun his mouth.

"Hungry are you?"

"I think I must have been born hungry. I don't remember ever having a full stomach. There were too many of us."

"Well, you can eat as much as you want here," said James. "There's no shortage of food though we're a little low on clothes to wear."

Roddy shrugged. "You have to be alive to wear clothes, and for that, you have to have food."

"Come and sit in, then," said Beth. She pulled up the stool to a space next to James. "You can sit here, Roddy." She pulled out her own chair and sat down. James joined her.

Roddy settled himself on the stool and reached for the biscuits and butter.

"Wait, you," said James. "We must say grace before we eat."

"What's grace?" Roddy withdrew his hand from the biscuits.

"We thank our heavenly father for the bounty he has set before us," said James. "Now bow your head and fold your hands."

"Heavenly Father, for what we are about to receive may we be truly grateful, and pardon our sins. In Jesus' name, amen."

James picked up his fork and looked at Beth who was looking at Roddy. He sat as still as a stone with his head bowed and his eyes closed. "It's okay Roddy, you can open your eyes now."

"Can I have a biscuit now?"

"Ladies first, then you may have one," said James. He picked up the plate and passed it to Beth. When Beth had taken the biscuit, James took one and passed the plate to Roddy. There were two biscuits left. He took them both then licked each one.

"Roddy, I know you're hungry, but it's not polite to take more than one of anything at a time. It's also not polite to lick your food before you eat it."

Roddy sat staring at the now empty plate. "But I don't want anyone to take the spare one, and what if there aren't anymore?"

"There are more in the pantry, and when those are gone I'll just make some more," said Beth.

Roddy sat staring at her with disbelieving eyes. "Really?"

"I'll show you." Beth rose from her seat, picked up the plate and carried it into the pantry. A moment later she was back with the plate over-flowing with biscuits. She set the plate on the table and sat down in her chair. "There! You see there are more."

Roddy swallowed his drool. "Are there more after that?"

Beth shrugged and picked up her spoon. "Not of this batch, but I'll make some more tomorrow. In the meantime, there's plenty of bread. Now eat before your supper is cold."

After supper, at which Roddy received several lessons in table manners, James said, "I want you to collect the eggs and then go to the barn with me to milk the cows."

"Eggs?" Roddy's eyes widened. "You have eggs?"

"Yes, dear, we sell them, and the egg man is due on Monday so I have to clean the eggs and get them ready for market."

"Can I have just one?" Roddy looked at Beth with big eyes.

"Of course you can. Two if you want two. I always save some back for us. Did you not have eggs at your home?"

"We only had two hens and a rooster so the eggs we did have went to Poppa because he needed his strength. Sometimes old Sadie would come by with a basket of eggs for us. We feasted then."

§

Beth made up a bed for Roddy on a straw pallet in the second room upstairs. That night after Roddy was asleep, she and James discussed the situation.

"I wonder how old he is?" said Beth.

"He cannot be more than nine or ten," said James.

"We need to contact his parents to let them know where he is."

"Eliza has family over that way. Maybe she knows who he is." James pulled his chair closer to the open oven door and drew the basket of broom straw from behind the stove and began tying it onto a long handle.

"Will she know even if we don't know his last name?"

"I think she will. There are only so many desperately poor families around."

"Aye," said Beth. "The poor ye shall always have with you. What if they don't want him back?"

"There's a good possibility they won't. It'll be just one more mouth to feed."

"Can we keep him? We have more than most, and you could certainly use the help."

James laughed. "Dear Beth, always looking out for the unfortunate. Of course he can stay here. Where else would he go?"

From upstairs they heard a quiet whoop of joy.

"Roddy, go to bed."

§

The next afternoon, Beth walked over to Eliza's. It was a brisk November day with a bit of wind that blew the thick grey clouds ahead of it. Beth climbed the steps and rapped on Eliza's back door.

"Ah, Beth, come in and welcome. To what do I owe this pleasure?" Eliza led the way to the kitchen and turned to take Beth's coat. "Pull a chair close to the stove and get warm." She hung Beth's coat behind the stove to warm for her return journey. "How is James?"

"James is thriving," said Beth, "as am I."

Eliza pushed the kettle over the heat, and it began to sing and popple to itself. "Have you been missing any more from your pantry lately?"

"Aye, I have," said Beth, "and we've caught the culprit."

"And who was it?"

"Not anyone we know. He's a runaway from Clyde River, so he says."

"Hm," said Eliza, "Clyde River."

"James tells me that you have family up that way and might know who he belongs to. He says his name is Roddy, and he's about ten or so."

"Did he tell you anything about his family?"

"Nothing except there are at least thirteen others, and they are desperately poor and hungry. The reason he left is because his father cussed at him once too often."

"That could only be Little Peter's children. Little Peter is great for swearing, and smacking too. His poor wife is terrified of him when he gets into one of his rages. He's kind of shiftless. Any money the older children earn gets taken to put food on the table."

"Does he drink?"

"I don't think so. He has never been fond of gatherings where there would be any."

"How could he lose a child and not miss him?" Beth pushed her chair a little farther from the stove.

"You've warmed up, then?" Eliza put the tea down to steep.

"I'm nice and toasty," said Beth.

Eliza sat down in the rocker again. "If he's Little Peter's son, I'm not sure that Peter even knows how many he's got, never mind where they are at any given time."

"He's that careless of his own?"

Eliza nodded. "He prefers to avoid the obvious, and poor Janet is so worn out, she can't keep up, so the children have taken care of each other from the time they could walk." She got up to get cups for the tea. "We'll have a little 'bonnick' and jam to go with our tea. It'll be tasty."

"I can't imagine having a child disappear and not wanting to know what had happened to him."

Beth sat shaking her head, her lips pursed.

"You've never experienced that kind of grinding poverty," said Eliza. "The neighbours share what they have when they have it to share, but they have children of their own to feed and clothe." She pulled a chair out from the table and went to pour the tea. "Sit in now for our little feast." She pulled up another chair. "What are you going to do with him?"

"I suppose I should let his mother know where he is. Even if she's too tired to worry, she should know that. James and I have decided to keep him. Roddy can help James about the farm, and I don't mind having a child around."

"You'll likely have one or two of your own soon."

Beth's face become rosy, and and her glance shied away from Eliza's inquisitive watchfulness. She felt the familiar lurch in her stomach at the thought of making babies. "I'm pretty old to start having children."

"Try and tell the *bairns* that."

CHAPTER FOUR

Beth walked home the long way through the woods. The path was soft with the needles of the spruces and the pines. The hardwood trees were bare of leaves, and she could see the expanse of the Northumberland Strait through the branches. Perching sparrows grew silent with her passing, and only the raucous cry of the ravens could be heard. The squirrels sat statue-still out of reach of the ground. The winter sun was growing heavy on the horizon as the day latened. Beth sang to herself as she walked along. Her cheeks grew rosy with the coldness of the wind.

I wonder if Roddy is Little Peter's son. If he is, I wonder if he'll want him back. Beth's mind rambled on. I've become quite fond of Roddy although he has only been with us a short time. She smiled, then frowned. I hope Little Peter doesn't want him back. I would miss Roddy, and he seems to be content to stay.

Her thoughts turned to what Eliza had said

about babies. She blushed again at the thought of a baby of hers and James'. I wonder could we? she thought. I'd like to have a little girl, or maybe a little boy. She chuckled to herself. It'd have to be one or the other. Her thoughts darkened as memories of home crowded into her mind. Her mood soon followed. How could we when I still haven't let James touch me? Poor James, such a wife as he's got. She sighed, then sighed again. I might as well put away these foolish thoughts. I'm too old to start having babies. She quickened her step and banished the wishful thinking from her mind.

"What did you find out from Eliza today?" asked James. He kept his voice low so that Roddy couldn't hear if he was listening.

Beth kept hers equally low. "She thinks he may be Little Peter's son. She said they're the poorest family in that area, and they have a number of children they don't keep very good track of."

"Hm," said James. He fell silent for a moment. "I suppose that the decent thing to do is to find out for sure and let them know he's here."

"Will they want him back?"

"I doubt it, if their household is in such disarray they may even be glad of having one less mouth to feed."

"How can we find out?"

"Send a note, I suppose." James picked up his pipe and tested the draw then began packing tobacco into the bowl. "I'll send it with Jack. He goes over that way often."

"It won't do any good," said Roddy from the loft. "They cannot read or write."

"Roddy, go to bed!"

"Can you read and write, Roddy?" Beth flapped the dishtowel to straighten it, then hung it on the rack behind the stove to dry.

"I ain't never been to school," said Roddy.

Beth sighed. "Ain't is incorrect; say, I have never been to school."

"I have never been to school," said Roddy. "Have you been to school, Beth?"

"Of course, both James and I have finished grade eight."

"Was it fun?"

"I don't think I'd call it fun exactly, but it was interesting." Beth pulled out a chair and sat down at the table, kitty corner from Roddy. "Do you know your ABC's?"

"What's that?" asked Roddy.

"They are the basis of any reading or writing you'll want to do."

"What if I don't want to read and write?" Roddy swung one foot idly beneath the table, making tapping sounds and making the salt and pepper containers rock and rattle.

"Roddy, reading and writing lie behind everything you do in life if you want to get ahead."

"Get ahead of what?" Roddy stopped swinging his foot and regarded Beth with bright blue eyes.

"If you want to earn money, you'll have to know how to read and write."

Roddy thought hard for a moment. "Poppa never earned any money, and that's why I had to run away."

"There, you see, if your Poppa had gotten an education, you wouldn't have had to run away."

"So how do I learn to read and write?"

"You go to school."

Roddy scuffed his shoe against the table leg. "I'm too old to go to school."

"Indeed you're not," said Beth. "As a matter of fact, if you are going to stay here, we will insist on you going to school."

"Oh," said Roddy. He tugged at a lock of his brown hair. "Can you teach me the ABC's?"

"Yes," said Beth. "If you want to learn." She opened the drawer in the table and took out a pad and a pencil. "Watch what I'm doing." She began writing the alphabet in block letters. "We'll start with these." She passed the pad of paper and the pencil to Roddy. "See if you can copy these like I've printed."

Roddy bent to his task, the pencil grasped tightly in one fist. His concentration was intense. The marks he made on the paper were ragged and crude compared to Beth's tidy printing. "There, is that what you mean?"

"Sort of," said Beth. "Try them again and make them tidier."

Roddy tried them again with more success. "Is that better?"

"It's better, but not good enough. They have to be as neat as mine."

Roddy sighed. "I don't know if I can make them that neat." He looked at his line of letters. He sighed again then returned to his task. In a few moments, he had drawn another line of letters.

"That's much improved, Roddy. Go to the head of the class." Beth patted Roddy on the back.

"Is that all there is to writing?"

"No, of course not. There are twenty-one other letters to learn. Would you like to learn a few more?"

Roddy sat up straighter. "Oh, yes. I want to learn them all."

"Maybe not in one day. Besides, you have to be able to say them in order. Can you do that?"

"You'll have to tell me the names."

Beth recited the first five letters in order. "Say them back to me."

Roddy recited them perfectly. "What are the next five?"

Beth wrote them out and said the names as she did so. "Now you do it." She handed the pencil back to Roddy.

Roddy laboured to recreate Beth's tidy printing. He put so much effort into the task that he broke the pencil lead. "I'm sorry, Beth. I didn't mean to break it." He cringed away from Beth as if she were going to strike him.

"Did you get swatted at home when you were doing your best?" Beth pulled the pencil out of Roddy's tight grip.

"Yes, ma'am. I was always getting smacked for something." Roddy sat as far away from Beth as he could manage without actually leaving his chair.

"We don't hit boys when they're doing the best they can." Beth rose to get a paring knife. "We don't hit boys at all." She opened the lid of the stove and shaved a new point on the pencil with the paring knife. She clattered the lid back into its place then handed the pencil to Roddy. "Don't hold it so tight. It's not going to run away." She sat down in her place again. "You only need to guide the pencil, and it's easier to control if you hold it more loosely."

Roddy relaxed his stranglehold on the pencil and copied his letters again.

"That's just about perfect," said Beth. "You're a quick study."

Roddy glowed. "Show me some more."

"Recite to me all the letters in order that I've shown you so far."

Roddy did so.

"That's excellent, Roddy. It's a shame you didn't have the opportunity to go to school when you were younger. You'd have been at the head of the class by now."

Roddy looked puzzled. "But I thought you said that I'm already at the head of my class."

Beth laughed. "The class here in this kitchen. I don't know where you'll fit when you go to school."

The porch door rattled as James joined them. "'Tis cold out there," he said. He shrugged out of his coat and hung it behind the stove. "We'll probably have snow by morning." He sat down at the other end of the table. "What are you two up to?"

"I'm learning my letters," said Roddy. "I'm going to learn to read and write." He pushed the pad over to show James. "D'you want me to recite them?"

James looked over Roddy's work. "Of course, I do." He sat back in his chair and folded his hands. "Let's hear them."

Roddy took a deep breath and recited the letters he had learned in order.

"Good on your head!" said James. "That was excellent. Your printing is coming along too, I see."

"I've written a note to Little Peter and his wife," said Beth. "I'm going to take it to Sandy. I heard he was going into town in the morning."

"You'd better hurry then. Sandy likes an early start."

"I hope he can find someone going to Clyde River who'll carry it the rest of the way." Beth folded the piece of paper and put it in an envelope.

"I hope Little Peter will be willing to let him stay with us. I've grown quite used to having a boy around the place," said James. "I'll miss him if he has to go back."

"I don't want to go back," said Roddy from the top of the stairs. "I'll run away again if he tries to make me."

James shook his head. "Roddy get down here!"

Roddy almost ran down the stairs. "Are you going to beat me?"

"I told you that we don't beat boys here unless they've been very disobedient," said Beth. "Now sit down. We have something we want to talk to you about."

Roddy pulled out a chair and sat down opposite

Beth and out of reach of James' big hands. "I'm not taking any chances." He stuck his lower lip out and stared at James.

James cleared his throat to keep from laughing out loud. "Roddy, this business of eavesdropping on other people's conversations has to stop."

"What's 'eavesdropping'?"

"It means listening in on others' conversations," said Beth.

"But how will I know what's going to happen to me?"

"When the time is right, we'll tell you what you need to know," said James.

"Oh," said Roddy. He was silent for a moment. "Then I guess I'll never know what's happening and when I need to hide."

"Get up, Roddy," called Beth from downstairs. "We're going to church today."

Beth heard Roddy's feet hit the floor and water being poured into the basin from the ewer on the stand. Soon Roddy came down the stairs still rosy from sleep. Beth set a bowl of porridge at his plate. "Have you ever been to church, Roddy?"

"Momma used to make us go to Sunday school some. I didn't like it."

"Well, we're going to make you go some more,"

said Beth. "Now eat your breakfast and get dressed. We only have an hour before church starts."

Roddy finished his porridge and drank the rest of the milk and sugar out of the bowl without the aid of a spoon. Beth rolled her eyes. "You and I have to have a talk about table manners very soon."

In time for the service, the little family set out down the track toward the church. Roddy raced ahead and found some treasure in the undergrowth at the side of the road. He stood there examining his find until James and Beth caught up with him.

"What did you find, Roddy?" asked James.

"A snake's eggshell, I think," said Roddy. He opened his hand to show them. It was a small blue speckled eggshell.

James looked at the shell closely. "That's a robin's eggshell." He looked up and began searching the bare tree limb. "We should be able to see the nest it fell from if we look hard enough."

"There it is," said Roddy. He pointed to a branch part way up the tree and out in the crook of the limb. "It looks deserted."

"It is November, after all. The birds have all flown south," said Beth. "We won't be seeing robins or any other migrating birds until spring." She continued down the track. "C'mon, we don't want to be late."

The remainder of the track was traversed in silence. Roddy skipped ahead and broke the rim of ice in the red mud puddles with his shoe.

"Roddy, don't mess about in the puddles," said Beth. "You'll be too dirty to take into church. Not only that, but you'll ruin your shoes."

"Momma never made a fuss about getting dirty on the way to church," said Roddy.

"I'm not your Momma," said Beth. "Now walk nicely."

Roddy fell into step with them and took Beth's hand. "I'll be good." He smiled up at Beth who couldn't help but smile back.

"G'day, James. Who's your company?"

"We're not sure," said James. "I found him sneaking loaves of bread from the pantry the other day and managed to capture him when he failed to jump the fence. He says his name is Roddy."

"Roddy, say g'day to Mr. MacDonald and shake hands," said Beth.

Roddy offered a somewhat grimy hand to Mr. MacDonald. "G'day."

"It's g'day, sir," said James.

"G'day, sir," said Roddy and withdrew his hand.

"We think he may be Little Peter's son from up west," said Beth. "I was talking to Eliza the other day, and she said that Little Peter had a number of children and didn't really keep track of them very well. I sent a note to Little Peter, but it's too soon to have heard back yet."

They watched Roddy hopping and skipping ahead of them. "You'll have your hands full," said Mr. MacDonald.

"Aye, we will that," said James.

"He's not a bad child," said Beth. "He's just full of energy."

When the church bell ceased tolling, people filed into the church. "Roddy, you come and sit with me," said Beth.

"Where's James going to sit?"

"He sits with the men on the other side. The children always sit with their mothers. Now come along, the service is about to start."

Beth took her seat with the women and children and bowed her head. She took Roddy's hand and pulled him onto the seat beside her. "Bow your head," she whispered to Roddy.

"Why?" Roddy whispered back.

"Because we say a prayer when we first come into church. Now be quiet." At least he whispered, thought Beth.

Presently the minister climbed to the pulpit and announced the first hymn. The congregation rose as one. The precentor announced the tune and sang the first line. The congregation straggled into the melody, following line by line what the precentor sang. It was sung with energy if not musicianship, and the music was greater than the sum of its parts.

Prayers were said, and other hymns were sung. The minister stood and pulled out his pocket watch and began to preach. The congregation settled into the pews, each person just so, knowing from years of sitting on the hard benches what would be the most comfortable position. It wasn't long before a gentle snore was heard in the background of the minister's words. Roddy turned around to look. Beth turned him around to face the front again. "Somebody went to sleep," said Roddy.

"That's Danny Jack," whispered Beth. "He's a very old man. Now sit still and be quiet."

Roddy sat swinging his leg and began making imaginary roads in the boards in the wall in front of him. Soon he began to swing the other leg too, tapping it against the pew ahead.

Beth put a firm hand on his knees. "Sit still!" she hissed at him.

Roddy tried to make himself small in the corner of the pew. He began counting the boards in the side wall. As the minister droned on, Roddy yawned and fought to stay awake to no avail. Beth looked across at him, and he was sound asleep. She left him asleep.

§

"That was a fine sermon, sir," said James. He shook hands with the minister at the door. "Will there be a meeting this week?"

"Aye, James, right after prayer meeting. We have some repairs to see to that have to be discussed."

Roddy followed James. He was still yawning and sleepy. "A fine sermon, sir," he said to the minister.

"Thank you, and I suppose you heard every word did you?" The minister's eyes twinkled.

"Aye, I did indeed," said Roddy and walked after James.

Beth rolled her eyes. "I believe he is going to be a handful," she said.

The sky had clouded over by the time they left the church.

"Come, Roddy, there's going to be snow before long," called Beth.

Roddy disengaged himself from the group of children he had joined and ran to Beth's side. "Geordie was telling me about the great sledding on the hill by his house. Can I go sledding at Geordie's?"

"Please," said Beth automatically.

"Please," said Roddy.

"Perhaps," said Beth. "If and when we get enough snow."

"How can you go sledding without a sled?" said James.

"Geordie might let me use his," said Roddy. He frowned. "He might."

"You'd better be sure he will," said Beth.

"I'd let him use mine if I had one."

The snow began to sift down, the flakes thin and far between at first.

"It's snowing!" Roddy ran in circles trying to catch snow flakes on his tongue. "I can go sledding soon."

"Let's see if we have enough snow first," said James. The snow flew thicker and faster. Roddy practically danced his way home in his excitement.

"I'd better put out the rope to the barn this afternoon," said James. "There's no telling how much snow we'll get."

"On the Sabbath?" said Beth.

"The better the day, the better the deed," said James. "I somehow doubt that the Almighty will fault me for protecting his own."

The snow continued all afternoon and into the evening. Roddy watched it accumulate. He was so anxious for the snow to build up, he kept running from window to window to watch it pile up.

Finally, after supper, James told him to go to bed.

"The snow will be there in the morning."

Roddy made one last trip from the pantry to the kitchen.

"Roddy!"

"I'm going. I just wanted one last look." He hurried up the stairs.

Beth and James sat in companionable silence. Shortly, James got up to put another log on the fire. "I hope the snow lasts long enough to satisfy Roddy's eagerness. It's not likely to this time of year."

"It's snowing pretty hard," said Beth. "It should stay until morning."

"I'll have to make him a sled too. It wouldn't be fair to give one to Robert's boy and not one to Roddy."

"You could give it to him for Christmas," said Beth. "Would you be able to get it done in time?"

"If I work on it in the evenings after he's gone to bed. I could sneak over to the smithy's after dark."

"I am going to make him some mittens. He'll need them when he goes out."

"If the snow keeps up, he'll need them before Christmas," said James.

The next morning the snow was just a patina of white over the red mud. Frost scored the window panes in paisley swirls and leaves. The sun rose over the line of spruce trees at the edge of the home field, turning the world sparkling silver. Roddy rubbed a peephole in the window frost and peered out into the sun bright morning.

"Aw, shucks! There's not enough snow to shovel, never mind go coasting."

"Roddy, what did James and I say about using bad language? Anyway, the winter hasn't even started. Come now and get your breakfast. James has already gone out to the barn, and you have to gather the eggs and fill the wood box before you even think about play."

Roddy took his place at the table, and Beth set a bowl of porridge in front of him. Roddy blew at the steam rising from the bowl and then piled a heaping spoonful of brown sugar on top before filling the bowl to the brim with milk still warm from the cow.

Beth shook her head. "I hope you're going to be able to manage all that." She set her own bowl of porridge on the table and sat down.

Roddy slurped at the edge of the bowl, then scooped a large spoonful of porridge into his mouth.

"Roddy, what did we say about stuffing your mouth full?"

"Mmf, glmff," said Roddy around the porridge. He slurped again at the milk in his bowl. "But

Beth, it's so good. We almost never had porridge. And when we did, there was never enough to go around, and Poppa always got the biggest share because he was the one who was working." He scooped up another spoonful almost as large as the first. "Is that better?"

"A little better, but you need to go smaller still."

Roddy glanced over his shoulder before taking a smaller bite. He scooped up a teaspoonful of porridge and milk. "Like that, Beth?"

"Much better." Beth watched Roddy eat. "Roddy, why do you look over your shoulder before you take a bite?"

Roddy shrugged one shoulder. "If I didn't guard it, someone might take it."

"Who would take your food from you?"

Roddy scraped at the bottom of his bowl. "One of the others. Usually Jack. He's bigger than I am, and if he took it, I knew I'd never get it back."

"Oh, Roddy." Beth pictured Roddy sitting at a table defending his breakfast from marauding siblings. It brought tears to her eyes, and she blinked them back. "What did the littlest ones do?"

"They never et much anyway. They was just there."

"'Never ate much' and 'were just there,'" said Beth.

CHAPTER FIVE

The snow lasted until mid-afternoon. As the sun reached each drift, its heat reduced the pile of snow to slush and water which gathered in the low points in the yard. Beth watched Roddy roll the wet snow into a lopsided snowman. After awhile, he came into the porch with his cheeks rosy red and his nose running. "Beth! Beth!" he called. "Can I have something to make eyes and nose for my snowman?"

Beth opened the porch door. "What kind of something?"

Roddy shrugged one shoulder. "I dunno, just something."

"Will a carrot do for a nose?"

Roddy's eyes opened wide. "A whole carrot just for the snowman?"

Beth rummaged in the bucket of carrots and found a short one. "Will this do?"

"It'll be perfect."

"You might look out by the woodpile and see if

there's anything there that'll work for eyes. You can ask James if he has a spare hat."

Roddy threw his arms around Beth's waist and gave her a slimy kiss on the end of her chin. "Thanks, Beth. You're so good."

Beth pulled out her handkerchief and wiped off her chin and then swabbed off Roddy's runny nose. "Use your handkerchief."

"Ain't got one."

"Haven't got one," said Beth. "Wait and I'll get one of James'."

"You haven't got one either?"

Beth laughed. "I've got one and James has one, but you don't. So wait and I'll get it for you." Beth went into the kitchen and came back in a moment with the handkerchief. "Now don't forget to use it." She tucked the cloth into Roddy's pocket.

She watched through the porch window as Roddy ran across the yard avoiding most of the puddles. His shoes need waterproofing. There'll be nothing left of them come Christmas, she thought, and Christmas is only a few weeks away. I must knit him a pair of mittens; those of James' are too big for him. A pair for James too. I'll have to see if Amanda has any yarn spun. She went into the warm kitchen and closed the porch door behind herself. There's that one closet left to turn out. I wonder what's in it. She opened the closet door and began lifting things out. In the far corner of the top shelf, she discovered a ball of pale wool with knitting needles stuck through the rounds of thread. Dangling from the loose end was a mitten cuff started, with numerous dropped stitches.

Beth took it out and dusted it off. Poor Amanda, she couldn't even do that right, she thought. She returned the contents of the shelf back in their place and sat down to unravel Amanda's work. I do believe that I have just enough to make Roddy a pair of mitts. James will just have to wait.

Preparations for Christmas went on in the evenings after Roddy was in bed and presumably asleep. James finished the sled for Roddy and had the smithy attach the metal runners. He hid it in the loft of the workshop. Beth finished the mittens and dyed them dark blue with dye from the crottle that she'd harvested off the spruce trees behind the barn. Lessons with Roddy went on apace. He was an apt learner and soon knew all his letters and could add and subtract simple sums. Spelling was his favourite lesson. Reading took some doing with only the Bible to read from, and so it was slow going.

"Would you like to have a Christmas tree, Beth?" James was mopping up the last of the gravy from his plate with a piece of bread.

"Do you have anything to decorate it with?" asked Beth

"What's a Christmas tree?" said Roddy.

"It's a tree that we cut from the woods and set up in the kitchen with decorations on it," said Beth. "I haven't had one since Momma died. Poppa said they were a waste of good trees."

"Amanda had some ornaments somewhere. There were only a few."

"I suppose we could make paper chains and popcorn balls. We could eat those after Christmas for a treat."

"Why would we do that?" asked Roddy.

"To celebrate Jesus' birthday."

"Oh," said Roddy. He bent over his plate, sopping up his gravy with his bread as he had seen James doing.

After dinner, James and Roddy went to the woods, and Beth popped popcorn. She managed to locate the box of ornaments in the cellar and brought them up to the kitchen. They were grimy with cobwebs and a patina of red dust. She washed each one carefully and laid them on a tea towel to dry. When James and Roddy came back with a tree, she had a yard of popcorn already strung.

"My goodness, look at you two," said Beth.

"Your faces are rosy, and even James has a runny nose. Is it cold out?" Beth peeled the hat and coat off Roddy and hung them behind the stove to dry. She rummaged in Roddy's pocket for his handkerchief and swabbed his streaming nose.

"It's cold enough," said James. "I think there's more snow on the way."

"Oh, goody," said Roddy. "Maybe I can go sledding at Geordie's house. Can I, Beth?"

"We'll see, said Beth. "In the meantime I need your help stringing this popcorn."

"Can I help too?" asked James.

Beth smiled. "Of course you can. Many hands make light work."

"I guess I'd better nail a stand to the bottom of the tree so you'll have someplace to put the string and the ornaments." James pulled on his sweater and went to the back porch to ready the tree for decoration.

By evening, the tree was decorated and standing in a corner of the parlour to keep it cool over the season.

"It's beautiful," said Roddy. His eyes were wide and sparkling with his excitement.

"You never saw a Christmas tree before," asked James.

Roddy shook his head. "We never had nothin'." He continued to gaze at the tree. "Does everybody have a tree?"

"Most people do," said Beth, "and the word is anything. We never had anything."

"Anything," said Roddy. "Does Robert have a Christmas tree?"

"Oh, yes," said James. "He even put candles on it a few years ago."

"Real candles?" Roddy drew a deep breath and contemplated what a tree would look like with candles on it. "Can we have candles on ours?"

"Not this year," said Beth. "I don't have any, and anyway they're a fire danger."

"Oh," said Roddy. "Maybe next year then."

"Maybe," said Beth.

Christmas Eve crawled nearer. Roddy was almost hopping in his excitement. "Would you like to cook a hen tomorrow?" asked James.

"That would be wonderful," said Beth. "I'll have to look and see if I have any summer savoury." Beth rose and began rummaging in the cupboard to see what she had. "I have almost a whole bag of savoury," she said. "You'll need to kill the hen today, then, if I'm to roast it tomorrow."

"I'll do it this morning," said James.

"Can I go too?" asked Roddy.

"If you want to, but it's not a pretty business." James pushed his arms through the sleeve of his coat and wrapped his scarf around his neck. "Get your coat on if you're coming with me." Together, Roddy and James set out for the hen coop. Roddy jumped icy red puddles and generally turned the walk to the barn into an adventure. Beth watched them go. I have never seen a child so easy to amuse as Roddy, she thought. Nothing is ever simple and straightforward with him. Everything is new and exciting every time he does it even if he's done it six times before. I'd better boil some water so they can defeather it.

After a few minutes, James and Roddy returned from the barn with the chicken dangling by its legs. Roddy was walking sedately now. A frown creased his forehead, and his voice was sober. "James, where do hens go when they die?"

"I don't know," said James, "to chicken heaven, I suppose."

"Where's chicken heaven?" Roddy hopped on one leg for a few steps. "Is it near to people heaven?"

"I'm not sure of that either. It's probably another chicken coop on the far side of heaven."

James opened the porch door and followed Roddy inside.

Beth came to the porch with a bucket of boiling water. "You'll need to take your coat off for this job, Roddy." She set the bucket on the floor. "Let me help you."

"I can do it myself," said Roddy.

"I know you can. I just like to help."

James hung his coat on the back of the door, pulled a leather apron on over his head and rolled up his sleeves. He dragged a three-legged stool over to the bucket. He picked up the hen and dipped her into the hot water and began to pull out her feathers.

"Can I try?" asked Roddy.

"Pull up a stool. It's hard work; d'you think you're strong enough?"

"Have you gutted it?" asked Beth.

"I did, but you'll need to clean it out and soak it overnight."

"I know. I've cleaned and roasted hens a few times. I'll soak it in salt water to get rid of the blood that's left, and it'll be ready for stuffing first thing in the morning."

"How're you doing there, Roddy?" asked James.

"I've pulled three feathers out already. Hens sure have a lot of feathers." He pulled out another one.

"Here, let me show you how. You'll be 'til midnight picking out one feather at a time." James took the hen from Roddy and began to strip the feathers by the handful. "Like this." He handed the hen back to Roddy.

Beth set the hen to soaking in salt and water that afternoon. "I think I'll make a raisin pudding for tomorrow while the fire's hot for supper."

"It'll be an early night for you, Roddy. You've had a busy day, and you want to give Santa enough time to come."

"What's a Santa?"

"He's known by names like Father Christmas, and he comes down the chimney with a sack filled with toys for good little girls and boys. But you have to go to bed and to sleep early. Santa likes to come after everyone's in bed."

"Even the grown-ups?"

Beth nodded. "Even the grown-ups."

"Bath first, then bed," said Beth.

Roddy took his bath without argument, his forehead wrinkled in thought.

"What are you thinking about, Roddy," asked Beth. She wrapped Roddy in a towel and began to rub him dry.

"I was wondering how good I have to be. I did some awful mean things this year."

"Like what?" asked James.

"Like running away from home, taking Maggie's doll from her and hiding it." Roddy chuckled. "She never found it for a week."

"I think Santa will overlook that since you realize that it's naughty," said Beth. "Santa's pretty forgiving."

"Like God?"

"Sort of," said Beth. She helped Roddy into

a clean set of James' long johns then rolled up the sleeves. "There now, enough talk. We'll read a passage and go to bed."

The next morning James went out to the work-shop early to retrieve the sled before Roddy came downstairs. James' breath circled his head like smoke before dissipating in the frigid air. Above, grey clouds gathered, heavy with snow. Crows rose, cawing, from the spruce trees behind the barn. James admired his handiwork on the sled then returned to the house.

"Any sign from Roddy?" James set the sled under the tree.

Beth shook her head. "Not yet, but breakfast is almost ready. You can call him."

She clanged the lid of the porridge pot and gave the porridge one last stir. James called to Roddy.

Roddy's feet hit the floor, and they soon heard water being poured into the basin, then a small yelp as the cold water came in contact with warm skin. In a few minutes, Roddy came down the stairs still warm and pink from sleep. He looked at the tree, and his eyes grew large as he saw the sled. "Ooh!" he said. "There really is a Santa." He crept closer to the tree. "And it's got my name on it!" He stretched out his hand to touch the wood. "Now I can go coasting with Geordie."

"There's something else under the tree with your name on it," said Beth. She pointed at the small parcel tied with the bright ribbons that had been used to tie her wedding bowls.

Roddy reached into the tree and pulled out the package. "It's so pretty. Can I open it?"

James nodded. "The tag says it's for you."

Roddy carefully untied the ribbon. "Mittens, just my size. How did he know?"

"I put a word in his ear a few weeks ago," said Beth.

Roddy tried on the mittens then began smoothing out the ribbons and winding them around his hand. A frown wrinkled his forehead.

"What's the matter?" asked James.

"I was just thinking how wee Maggie would love to have some ribbons for her hair." He continued winding the ribbon until he had a neat ball. "How could I ever get them to her?"

"You save them, and in the spring, we'll go and visit your family."

"I dunno. It's an awful long way."

"We'll take the horse and wagon," said James. "Maybe Beth will come too."

"It'll be nice to see wee Maggie again. I teased her a lot but I miss her now."

The snow began again that afternoon. By nightfall, it had transformed the yard to a muffled whiteness and capped the fence posts and tree branches. And still it snowed.

James melted a peep hole through the frost on the window glass with his warm finger. "I'm glad I set the rope to the barn and fed the animals early. This storm means business this time."

"Aye, well, there'll be enough snow for Roddy to go coasting on," said Beth.

"He'll be right happy." James propped his feet on the open oven door. "What do you think of going to see Roddy's parents in the spring?"

"I'm not sure," replied Beth. "They may want to keep him."

"Maybe." James shrugged. "Would that be such a bad thing?"

Beth swallowed hard against the lump that suddenly formed in her throat at the thought of losing Roddy. "I'd miss him."

"And so would I," said James. "He brightens the days with his questions and his curiosity. He's into everything."

"We haven't heard a peep from his *faither*, and it's been almost two months."

"Oh, aye, I know. But neither one knows how to write, and we're not likely to hear until spring now."

"If I had a missing child, I'd look for him night and day until I found him," said Beth. "If I had even one of my own I'd make home such an inviting place he wouldn't want to run away."

James chuckled. "You'd spoil it, eh?"

"Is that what I'd do?" Beth thought over the consequences of spoiling a child and frowned. "Yes, I guess that's what I'd do—if I had one of my own."

James swung his feet from the oven door and gathered Beth into his arms. "Would you like to have one of your own, *mo graidh*?"

"Aye, I would," replied Beth, "though I'm getting kind of old."

"Not too old," said James. He dropped a kiss on top of Beth's brown head. Her hair was starting to show some grey strands.

"Not yet, but soon." Beth thought briefly about the creating of infants. She shivered and thrust the thought out of her mind. She stirred in James' arms.

"What is it, my darling?"

"A goose walked on my grave," said Beth and pulled away from James.

James thought of the several times that he and Beth had tried to be husband and wife, how she had shuddered in just the same way and rolled away from him as soon as she could. She didn't used to be so stand-offish, thought James. My sweet Beth used to be so warm and giving I had a hard time not to bring shame on her.

"It's more than a goose," said James, "I think it

must be the whole flock."

Beth sniffed, then rummaged in her pocket for her handkerchief.

James tilted her face up to where he could see it in the light from the lamp. "Are you crying, *mo graidh?*"

Beth ducked her head and mopped at her tears.

James tried to take her into his arms again. "Hush, my sweet. It can't be as bad as all that."

Beth freed herself from James' embrace and took a pace or two in the small kitchen. She thought of all that had been done to her after her mother had died, and the tears came in a flood. She swabbed at them to no avail.

"Whatever is wrong, my dear?" James tried to put his arms around Beth, but she pushed him away. He dropped his arms and tried to follow Beth in her pacing. There was not enough room. At last, Beth sat down in the rocker and began to rock wildly.

James knelt beside her and took her hand in his calloused fingers. "Tell me what it is, Beth, maybe I can help."

"No one can help. What's done is done." She began to sob again. "'Twas just plain evil what he did."

"He who?"

"Poppa." Beth sniffed hard and swiped at her nose again. "He was smart enough not to try anything while Momma was around, but as soon as she was out of the house, he was after me. I tried to hide from him, but I couldn't. He always found me or waited until I came out from where I hid. After Momma died, I had no defence. I used to try to pretend I was asleep, but he always woke me up." Beth sniffed hard against a fresh spate of tears. "Many nights I took my pillow and a blanket and slept in the far corner under the bed. I was very familiar with the underside of that bed." Beth began to sob hard again.

James sat back on his heels. "So that's what he meant. That bastard!" He patted Beth's arm. It was all he could reach of her. "That filthy bastard." James barely spoke above a whisper. "What about your brothers?"

"I don't know. They were only little when Momma died. Samuel tried to touch me when he was a teenager, but I threatened him with the butcher knife and he never did it again. He was always a lot of noise and not much action."

James shook his head. "Thank goodness for that." He took Beth's hand and raised her to her feet. "You know, *mo graidh*, that I would never deliberately hurt you. You know that, don't you?" He gathered her into his arms and stroked her greying hair and wiped the tears from her cheeks with his calloused thumb. Gradually Beth relaxed into his arms. "I know, but 'tis hard to do that without remembering."

§

James left for the barn early the next morning holding onto the rope he had tied between the house and the barn. The snow was still drifting and piling in unexpected places, and the wind in its strength tore the door out of James' hand and slammed it hard enough to shake the house. Beth startled and went to peer out into the whiteness through the peep hole James had made earlier on the frosty kitchen window. We're in for more snow yet, she thought. I'm glad we have all that food put by and that James put the woodpile so near the house. We won't go cold or hungry. She heard the thump of Roddy's feet and his gasp as they hit the cold mat beside his bed. In a few minutes a mop-haired Roddy clambered down the steep stairs from the sleeping loft.

"Where's your sweater? It's cold in here this morning." Beth pulled a chair closer to the stove and opened the oven door. "Sit here and get warm while I fix your porridge." She bustled about getting Roddy's breakfast. She ladled a hearty serving of oatmeal out of the pot on the stove and poured some milk on it and scraped some sugar off the loaf over the top. She handed the bowl to the still shivering Roddy. He huddled by the oven door and began spooning hot porridge and milk into his mouth.

Beth poured him a cup of tea, added milk and set it on the stove top beside him.

Roddy looked up from his porridge bowl. "Real tea?"

"Yes, real tea, but we won't be making a habit of it," said Beth. "It's too cold this morning for milk."

Roddy tipped the porridge bowl up and drank the remaining milk from it. He then sat looking at the steaming mug of tea. "I've never had real tea before."

"You haven't?" Beth's surprise showed in her raised eyebrows. "Not even a sip from your father's cup?"

Roddy shook his head. "We only had tea on special occasions and then only a taste. Sometimes it was only Poppa who had any." Roddy picked up the mug of tea and sniffed at it. He wrinkled his nose, took a careful sip, then another. Soon the mug was empty.

"Well, what did you think?"

Roddy shrugged. "It was kind of bitter, but I guess I could get used to it." His shivering ended in a small shudder. He was silent while Beth put away the breakfast things. He watched Beth at her work, then said, "I heard you crying last night. Are you not well?"

Beth looked at him and blinked. "It's nothing you need concern yourself with, Roddy." She drew her lips into a thin line of severity.

"I heard you talking about your *faither* and your brothers." Roddy persisted. "Did they hurt you?"

"My *faither* did, but that's a long time ago." Beth took up the broom and began to sweep vigorously. "He cannot hurt me any longer."

Roddy got up from his chair by the oven door and put his skinny boy arms around Beth's waist. "If he ever tries to hurt you again, I'll protect you, Mother."

Tears sprang to Beth's eyes and almost spilled over. She returned Roddy's hug. "You called me Mother."

"Don't you want me to call you Mother?" Roddy looked up at Beth with wide eyes. "You are the only mother I have now."

Beth hugged him again. "Of course, you may call me Mother. I am honoured."

Roddy released himself from Beth's arms and picked up his mug. "May I have some more tea, please?"

Beth thought about having her own child almost all morning. Sometimes her heart lifted with the joy of the idea, and other times sadness was upon her at the remembrance of what her father had done and what her brothers had tried to do. If only I had married James in the first place, she thought. Tears sprang to her eyes, and she blinked them back. I hope James can forgive me. My heart is aching that I cannot come to him pure and free from the sin and shame of it. Maybe he won't want children with me now that I've told him the truth. Tears escaped her vigilance this time. Oh, it would be so sad to never have a family and all because of Poppa. She mopped at the wetness on her cheeks, concealing the tears behind the pretence of a runny nose. James was so understanding last evening; I hope he doesn't reconsider. He won't, she reminded herself. He's such a good man. She took a deep breath and straightened her shoulders. I must stop this mooning and moaning. What's done is done, and what will be will be. She blew her nose again and swallowed hard, but the lump in her throat and the sadness in her heart persisted.

In the days that followed, Beth steeled herself against imagining a child of her own.

'Tis no good to get my hopes up, she thought. She threw herself into a spate of housekeeping to keep her mind occupied. She cleaned the already spotless kitchen and turned out neat cupboards and inventoried her supplies. Her appetite began to fail until James noticed her pallor and thinness.

"Beth, what's troubling you so?" he asked. Roddy was outside playing in the snow building snow caves, and they had the kitchen to themselves.

"I'm fine," said Beth. "I'm just thinking about the spring and how we promised Roddy that we'd take him to see his family when the roads were fit, that's all."

James looked at her face trying to discern the truth of her reply. "Is that really all it is?" He continued to watch her as she ran the hot iron over James' Sunday shirt.

"What if they want him back?" She set the iron back on the stove with force and flapped the shirt to straighten the sleeves. "What'll we do without him?" A tear ran down her cheek and dripped off her chin onto the ironing board. "We'll have no child at all."

James reached across and patted her hand. "First of all, Beth, I don't think that's likely to happen. If they'd wanted him back, they'd have come and got him before now. I think except for the formalities, he's ours to raise." He pulled his handkerchief from his back pocket and handed it to Beth. "Are you sure that's all you're on about?"

"Would you miss him if they did want him back?" Beth sniffed back more tears.

"I would, indeed," said James. "The little fellow really brightens the day with his energy and his questions and his imaginings. I've never seen such a busy mind."

Beth managed a weak laugh. "He does keep

life entertaining doesn't he?" She swabbed at her damp nose once more and handed the handkerchief back to James.

"You know, Beth, maybe we should be thinking about one of our own," said James. He watched Beth as she turned and picked up another garment to iron.

Beth kept her face half turned from him as she arranged the shirt on the board and picked up the iron. "Do you really want a child with the likes of me?" Her voice rose from the distress of the question.

James leaped from his seat and came around to where he could look Beth in the face. "The likes of you?! What kind of a question is that?"

Beth ducked her head and began to cry again. "I don't see how you can look at me after hearing what my father did."

James took her hands in his and drew her out from behind the ironing board. "Beth ... , Beth ..." He cleared his throat. "Beth, my darling, you are my chosen one no matter what your father has done. He's the one who has done it, not you. I loathe the man for his evil, but I remind myself that he will reap his reward. The likes of you, indeed!" He pulled Beth into his arms and smoothed her hair with his work-roughened hands. "I wish I'd had the sense and the strength to take you away when your mother died."

"You'd have been too late already," said Beth. "He started as soon as I was old enough." She pulled away from James.

"D'you mean when you were a child?" James' face settled into a fierce scowl, and he began to pace the confines of the kitchen.

Beth nodded. "As soon as I started growing up, he couldn't keep his hands to himself. And it only got worse from there."

"Where was your mother in all of this?" James came to a halt in front of Beth.

"Momma didn't seem to know. In the beginning, it was just touches and slaps and tickling. He was careful to not do anything in front of her. Then when he got bolder, he threatened me into silence by saying what he'd do to Momma if I told her. It was awful. I was so scared." Beth shuddered at the remembrance of it. "So, of course, I never told her." She wrapped her arms around herself and rocked back and forth. "I don't know to this day if she ever even guessed. I am so ashamed." Beth was silent for a few minutes, still wrapped in her arms and rocking. "When Momma got sick, it just got worse. When you and I were engaged, she was so excited. I sometimes thought then that she knew and saw that as a way out of the situation, but I don't know for sure." It was Beth's turn to pace. "After Momma died, he was after me all the time."

"And that's why you ran away."

Beth collapsed onto the lounge. "That's why I ran away."

CHAPTER SIX

Beth struggled with a heavy heart for several weeks. James was extra gentle and helpful to her and sometimes in the evening just held her silently and caressed her head with his big work worn hands. Beth was grateful for his comfort and sometimes cried when she was alone that she could not bring herself to be more of a wife to him. At last when she could grieve no more, she made a decision. 'Tis not fair to James that I deny him his comfort just because of what my father did. I have to get over my distaste and squeamishness. I will tell him this evening after Roddy goes to bed.

Thankfully, Roddy went up to bed with no protest that evening. Beth checked on him a half hour later, and he appeared to be sleeping. She climbed back down the steep stairs and fussed around the kitchen for a few minutes. "Would you like some tea, James? There's still a drop left from supper."

"Is there enough for two?"

Beth shared the remains of the pot between two mugs and handed one to James. "That shouldn't keep us awake." She sat down next to James who was lying on the lounge. He moved onto his side to make room for her. She sighed and then sighed again, staring at her half full mug.

"What's troubling you, Beth?" James swallowed his tea in a couple of gulps and set his mug on the side table.

Beth hesitated and sipped at her tea once more. She was silent for so long that James thought she was not going to answer.

"Beth?"

"I heard you. I was just thinking of the finality of what I want to say and what it will mean to us."

James frowned. "What could be so final as all that?"

"I have been thinking a lot about what I told you a few weeks ago and what we said, and I've come to a decision."

"Oh?"

"Yes." Beth took a deep breath. "I have decided that I will try to be a proper wife to you because 'tis not fair to you that I be so frightened. You shouldn't have to pay for what my *faither* did." She took another deep breath. "If I cannot be a proper wife to you I want you to divorce me, and find another who will." She could feel her heart breaking in her chest and, oh, it hurt.

James gasped at her statement. He struggled to a sitting position and put his arms around Beth. "You are a proper wife, my precious. I don't want any other, no matter what happens."

Beth heard the tears in his voice, looked up at him and began to cry too. "I am so glad you think that. I don't know what I would do without you now." She turned her face into the bib of his overalls and sobbed harder. She could feel his tears dropping silently onto her head.

James tipped her chin up so that he could see her face. "You believe me, don't you?"

Beth sniffed deeply and scrubbed at her wet cheeks. "I believe you, and I am so grateful."

James clicked his tongue. "'Tis not necessary to be grateful. You are my wife and the only one I want."

They consummated their marriage that night, and Beth cried again for the sweetness of it.

Spring hesitated its way into the end of March, and by April, the trees were beginning to look as if they might be considering breaking into leaf. The few flowers that James had planted for Amanda poked through the hard red clay next to the sun-warmed foundation and provided tiny spots of colour here and there. There was still frost at night. Beth lost her worried look, and her cheeks took on a tiny flush of pink. She laughed occasionally and seemed to have more energy. James watched her and was gratified.

I'm so glad it's finally spring, thought Beth. It's almost time to get on with spring housecleaning. She snapped the dish towel, folded it and hung it on the rack behind the stove to dry. The first warm day … her thoughts strayed to her changed circumstances, and she smiled. It's wonderful to be keeping house for James instead of Poppa and the boys. It must be filthy over there by now. She shuddered at the thought. Poor Momma would be horrified at the state of her home. She was always so proud of it. I'm thankful I'm out of there. She thought of her life with James and all its facets and blushed. I'm so glad I … she let her thoughts linger briefly on her and James' changed relationship. He's so happy these days. I hear him whistling as he goes about the farm no matter how hard the task. Roddy seems happier too. I guess it rubs off on us all. I'm glad Roddy's doing so well in school. He's a smart little fellow and loves to learn. He might make something of himself someday if we can give him the chance. Her happy mood sagged. If his *faither* and *maither* don't want him back.

§

At last the weather turned warm enough to be outside with just a sweater on. The planting was nearly completed, and Beth had planted her vegetable garden after James had worked the clay with the horse and plough. The house sparkled inside, and everything was tidy inside and out. Beth looked around herself with satisfaction.

James came in from the barn, banging the door behind himself. He dropped a kiss on Beth's cheek and began rummaging around the pantry for something to eat.

"James, go sit down, you're making a mess of my nice clean pantry. I'll make you a *strupach*." She pushed the kettle over the fire to boil for tea and bustled around the pantry tidying after James' mess as she went. Soon she had a plate of bread and molasses, and a plate of cookies on the table, and the tea was steeping.

"D'you think that'll keep you 'til dinner time?" She pulled out a chair and sat down across the table from James.

James spooned molasses onto a slice of bread and butter. "I think so." He took a bite and slurped at the molasses running over the side of the bread. "If not, I'll be back," he said around a mouthful. He swallowed and said more clearly, "You know, Beth, we should soon take Roddy to see his family and find out what they want to do with him."

Beth's heart seemed to fall to her boots. She

rose, scraping her chair across the floor and went to busy herself pouring tea for them. She came back to the table carrying two mugs and set one down in front of James.

"You're looking very worried," said James.

"I am. I've been trying not to think of them wanting him back. What if they do?"

"I know, I've been trying not to think of it either." He reached across the table to pat her hand. "But we'll never rest easy if we don't know, and wouldn't you rather know than not know?"

"Sometimes I think I'd rather just go on as we are." Beth's eyes filled with tears. "If we have to give him back, this house will be so empty."

"Would you like to go and see your family this Saturday, Roddy?" Beth held her breath waiting for his answer.

Roddy considered the offer for at least a minute, it seemed. "I dunno, I guess so." He frowned and then smiled a little. "I'd like to see wee Maggie again and bring her the ribbons for her hair." He fell silent again. Then he said, "I won't have to stay, will I?"

"No, not unless your *pàrants* insist," said Beth.

"They won't," said Roddy. His tone was very sure.

"How can you be so certain?" asked James. "You are their child."

"Poppa always said I was good for nothin'
and then he'd take a swipe at me with whatever
he had in his hands. He used to hit us all, even
wee Maggie."

"Did he hit your *maither*, too?"

"She was the only one he didn't hit because he
knew she'd hit him back, and he'd get the worst
of it. He tried it once when I was little, and she
came after him with the frying pan and hit him
on the head. Near knocked him out. I hid out in
the barn for hours after that. Wee Maggie and I."

Beth and James exchanged glances. Beth shook
her head. "How old were you then?"

"Just little. Wee Maggie had barely learned to
walk, and I had to carry her piggyback to get her
into the loft. She was crying and so scared she
messed herself, and she smelled to high heaven.
And I couldn't do anything about it." Roddy
looked very distressed. "I was so ashamed that
I couldn't help her."

"You got her out of there. That was certainly a help," said Beth. "Are you much older
than Maggie?"

"Dunno," said Roddy, "a year or two maybe."
He squirmed on his chair. "Can I go out and play
now, Beth?"

Beth helped him into his sweater. He pulled
on his own boots.

"Don't go far," said James. "It's getting cool out

and almost time for the sun to go down."

"Won't," said Roddy going out and slamming the door behind himself.

"Can you believe it?" said Beth. "Imagine treating a toddler like that!"

"Imagine treating anyone like that," said James.

"We can't let him go back to that; it's criminal."

"It's not, but it should be." James was silent for a moment. "If they don't want him back, d'you want to try for wee Maggie too?"

"Oh, James, could we? He sets great store on her, and it would be nice to have a little girl around too."

"What about one or two of our own, too?" asked James.

Beth ducked her head and blushed a rosy red.

Saturday morning, James and Roddy hitched Tidy to the wagon, and Beth packed a lunch.

"Have you got your list for the store?" asked James.

"Oh," said Beth, "I've been so distressed about them maybe wanting Roddy back that I left it on the sideboard." She scurried back into the house and retrieved the list.

Roddy perched himself on the seat between James and Beth. "You know they won't want me back," he said with certainty in his voice.

"Maybe they will after they've seen what a fine young man you've become," said Beth and sniffed back the instant tears.

Roddy flung his arms around Beth's neck and gave her a sloppy kiss on her cheek. "Don't you worry, Mother, they won't."

James clucked to Tidy and slapped the reins gently on her rump and they were on their way, the iron wheels crunching and grinding across the occasional patch of red sandstone and the gravel on the road. The day was becoming warmer as they rolled toward the barge that would take them across the Hillsborough River to Charlotte-town. The sky was clear but for a few shepherd's clouds, and the breeze was from the south. The trees were becoming close to being in full leaf but were still a bright spring green. Birds tried to conceal themselves and their new-made nests behind the still inadequate foliage, and squirrels scolded their passage from safe branches. Green grass was poking through the dried grass of last fall. It was altogether a glorious day.

Beth's heart was heavy, and she and James were silent, and as a consequence, so was Roddy. As they turned onto the Harbour Road, Roddy said, "Sing to us, Beth, I mean, Mother. I love to hear you sing."

Beth gave him a hug. "What'll it be then?"

"Sing 'Speed Bonny Boat'."

"Good choice," said James.

Beth sang all the verses in her rich soprano. James joined in on the chorus, his bass voice a suitable contrast to Beth's. Roddy rocked back and forth and crooned along with them in an undertone.

"D'you know what that song's about, Roddy?" asked Beth when she'd finished the last chorus.

Roddy shook his head. "No, but 'tis mighty pretty."

"It's all about Bonny Prince Charlie escaping from the English army in Scotland. He lived on the Isle of Skye for awhile where a lady by the name of Flora MacDonald hid him. It's quite an adventure. You'll learn about it in school."

"Oh," said Roddy. "Sing it again, Beth."

Beth sang it again and then once more, and by then, they were almost to the river.

James pulled the horse and wagon into line with the other wagons and tied the reins. He jumped down and went to talk to a group of men waiting to cross the river. Beth and Roddy climbed down and went for a walk to the river's edge.

"How do we get across, Beth?" Roddy stood and stared over the width of the river.

"There's a barge that takes us."

"What's a barge?"

"It's a big, flat bottomed boat with room on it for several carts and horses and passengers. There's a bench for people to sit on as they go across. There aren't any sides so I want you to sit on the bench with me. No running around."

"So it's kind of like a big raft?"

Beth nodded then looked down at Roddy. "How'd you get across the river when you came our way?"

"There weren't one the way I came. Just a lot of marsh. I got my feet wet. It took me a day and a half to get my shoes dry, and then they fell apart."

"You must have gone across at the head of the river, did you?"

"Dunno," said Roddy. "All I know is that it was dark and wet."

"Why'd you go in the dark?"

"Didn't want no one to see me." Roddy pointed out to the middle of the river. "Look, Beth, is that the barge?"

Beth followed Roddy's pointing finger with her eyes. "That's it."

"C'mon, let's hurry, we don't want to miss it."

Beth laughed. "It's still only half way across. I doubt we'll miss it."

"But we might," said Roddy.

Soon the barge was tying up next to the dock. The carts were unloaded and the ones waiting were loaded on and the uneasy horses tied. James stood at Tidy's head to reassure her. Roddy sat with Beth on the bench. Too soon for Roddy, they were across the river and tying up on the other side.

"That was fun," said Roddy. "Can we do it again sometime?"

"Sooner than you think," said James. He boosted Roddy onto the wagon seat again and helped Beth over the wheel, then climbed on himself.

"Maybe we should stop at the store and get something to take with us," said Beth.

James nodded. "I brought a little extra money with me just for that."

"You're a good and kind man, James," said Beth.

They stopped at the store and purchased a fifty pound bag of oatmeal, a fifty pound bag of flour and a gallon of molasses for Roddy's family and were on their way again. Too soon they were turning into the lane that led to Roddy's house. The lane was long and a strip of grass grew down the middle. The ruts were filled with red mud and puddles. Tidy pulled hard through the mire. Weeds and blueberry bushes grew along the broken down fence along the edge, and early dandelions and devil's paintbrush dotted the cow pasture on the other side. The single cow raised her head and looked at them, then returned to her meagre grazing. They entered the yard.

"Whoa, Tidy," said James. He pulled on the

reins, and Tidy came to a halt near the porch door. Several dirty children stood in a half circle at the end of the porch, looking at them without saying anything. One little girl stood apart sucking on her finger, her bare feet curling themselves into the sand of the dooryard. Her lank blondish hair hung in strings around her face and in her eyes. She looked to be about five or six.

"That's wee Maggie," whispered Roddy. "She hasn't grown much since last spring."

"What is she doing out on her bare feet on a cool day such as this?" said Beth.

"She don't have no shoes."

Beth felt a lump rise in her throat. "Poor wee Maggie."

James climbed down from the wagon and went around to assist Beth down. Roddy jumped down on his own and went to stand in front of Maggie.

"D'you remember me, Maggie?" he asked. There was a trace of anxiety in his voice.

Maggie stood and stared at him in silence still sucking her finger. Suddenly she popped her finger from her mouth and threw her arms around Roddy's neck. "Roddy! Where has you been? I couldn't find you, and I cried and cried."

Roddy returned her hug with enthusiasm. "Come and meet Beth and James. They've looked after me all winter, and now they've brought me to see you." He took Maggie's hand and drew her toward where Beth and James were trying to make friends with the other children to no avail.

Roddy tugged at Beth's sleeve. "This is wee Maggie, Beth." Maggie hid behind Roddy and peered at the strangers.

Beth knelt down to Maggie's level and held out her hand. "Don't be afraid Maggie; I won't hurt you."

Maggie came a little way from behind Roddy but clung to his arm lest Beth try to grab her.

Behind Beth, the door opened, and a scrawny woman almost as grimy as the children came onto the porch. She was great with child. "You kids scat." She waved the broom she held in her hands in the direction of the line of children as if they were little animals. The children fled. Maggie held onto Roddy and tried to hide behind him away from her mother's threatening broom.

"Are you folks lost?"

"Not really. Are you Roddy's mother?"

"Aye, I see you have the scoundrel with you. He ran away last summer, and we didn't know where he was. We figgered he'd hopped on one of them sailing ships bound for Montreal or the Boston States and we wouldn't see him again." She turned to Roddy. "Are you come home to stay, then."

"That's actually why we're here." James cleared his throat. "Roddy has been living with us since late last fall, and we've become very fond of him so we'd like to keep him with us. My wife and I have none of our own, and we'd miss him if he couldn't stay with us."

The woman's eyes narrowed as she took in the loaded wagon and Roddy's neat trousers and sweater. "I'll sell him to you."

Beth's eyes widened in surprise. "Sell ..." she began, but James nudged her, and she clamped her mouth shut on the remainder of her sentence.

James pursed his lips and considered the offer. "I don't hold with buying and selling humans. There's been too much of that in the world as there is, but if you'll throw in wee Maggie here, I'll give you the contents of the wagon for them."

The woman's eyes lit up at the abundance of the trade. The wagon was full to overflowing. "Done," she said.

James turned and began unloading the wagon. Roddy gave Maggie into Beth's care and went to help him.

Beth knelt again to Maggie's height. "D'you want to come home with Roddy and live with us?" she asked.

Maggie considered this for a moment still sucking on her finger. "Can I sleep with Roddy?"

"You may share a room for now, and maybe later on, you'll want a room for yourself next to Roddy's."

"Okay," said Maggie and resumed sucking on her finger.

Beth turned to her mother and asked, "How old are Roddy and Maggie?"

"Oh, gorsh, let me think." She counted backward on her fingers. "Roddy was nine last fall and Maggie'll be seven in the spring. I don't recall the dates. I have twelve others and another one on the way. It's hard to keep up." She continued to watch as Roddy and James carried the bags and boxes of supplies into the house. "That's a fine trade we've made," she said.

Beth raised her eyebrows behind the woman's back.

In a few minutes, the truck wagon was empty. James helped Beth onto the seat, and Roddy climbed onto the tail of the wagon and hoisted Maggie up beside himself. "I'll ride back here with Maggie," he said. "I don't want her to fall off."

"Don't you fall off either, then," said Beth.

James turned Tidy around and then climbed up next to Beth, and they started out the lane.

"That was clever of you," said Beth. "Getting her to 'throw in' Maggie for the whole wagon load."

"I'd have given her the whole load just for Roddy, but it seemed like a way to get Maggie for him like he wanted. They've missed each other, I think."

They travelled in silence for several miles. Once

or twice Beth looked back to check on Roddy and Maggie. They were perched on the tailgate as close as they could get to each other. Maggie continued sucking her thumb, the only part of her that could be called remotely clean. Beth could hear Roddy telling Maggie what to expect once they got home.

"Beth will expect you to wash your face and hands every morning and brush your teeth and take a bath every Saturday. She'll make your dresses and wash and iron them too. You'll have to help her do things around the house like I help James around the farm. She's very kind and gentle, not like Momma. I call her Beth most of the time, but on special occasions, I call her Mother. James is not like Poppa either. He will never hit us or call us names. He expects us to mind though and to mind Beth too. And almost best of all, there's lots to eat."

Beth smiled and nudged James. "Are you listening?" she whispered.

James stifled a chuckle. "I sure am. I think Roddy thinks he's died and gone to heaven."

"And now we've come to rescue Maggie," said Beth. She looked behind once more. Maggie's head was on Roddy's shoulder, and her thumb had fallen out of her mouth. She was fast asleep. Roddy was still talking.

§

They stopped at the store again to replenish their supplies and were soon on their way to the barge. Maggie clung to Roddy as if she were afraid of losing him. When James pulled Tidy to a halt at her place on the barge, Maggie refused to get down from the wagon and would not let go of Roddy.

"It's alright, Maggie," said Roddy. "I won't leave you." He pushed himself back farther on the tail board. "If we stay here and stay still, we won't fall in the water."

Maggie's face lost some of its look of terror, but she clung to Roddy with both hands, her soggy thumb forgotten in her fear. The barge bumped away from the wharf. Maggie let out a little yelp.

Beth came over and stood by her other side. "I'll just stand here on this side, and Roddy and I will keep you safe." Beth turned her head and wrinkled her nose as the odour of unwashed child rose from Maggie. "We'll have to get you bathed before you go to bed this evening. I'll find you a nice clean nightie and a pretty nightcap. Will you like that?"

Maggie stared at Beth and nodded slowly.

"Say thank you, Beth," said Roddy.

"Thank you, Beth," said Maggie and continued to stare.

Beth smiled down at Maggie. "You're very welcome, Maggie. I hope you'll like living with Roddy and us. There are new kittens in the barn. I just saw them last evening when I went out to get the milk from James. The old mother cat had three grey striped ones and two orange and white spotted ones. She has kept them in hiding since they were born a few weeks ago. They're a little wild so you'll have to be gentle with them and tame them. You can help me gather the eggs tomorrow morning. Roddy can do it this evening while we get you nice and clean and pretty." Beth chatted their way across the river to distract Maggie and soon they were tying up on the other side. The sun was just dropping behind the trees behind the barn when they arrived home.

Roddy and James unloaded the wagon, and Beth put things away. Maggie sat on the lounge sucking her thumb and staring at all the activity. Her odour slowly pervaded the kitchen. Beth wrinkled her nose. "I need you to bring me the tub, and I think you and Roddy had better do your barn work before supper." She stirred up the remaining coals in the stove and added some kindling and a piece of wood. She pushed the kettle over the hottest part of the fire, and it began to groan and sing, quietly at first, then on to a full boil.

At last everything was arranged in the pantry

to Beth's satisfaction. James and Roddy dragged in the big wash tub then disappeared in the direction of the barn. Beth tested the water in the tank on the end of the stove. She dipped water from the tank into the tub and added the water in the kettle to bring it up to bathing temperature.

"Come, then, Maggie, let's get you bathed and into a clean night shirt." Beth held out her hand to Maggie. Maggie shrunk back into the corner of the lounge. "What's wrong, Maggie? Are you afraid of getting in the bathtub?"

Maggie nodded slowly.

"Why?"

"Might drown," whispered Maggie and stuck her thumb back into her mouth.

"You won't drown," said Beth. "I'll be right here. I won't let anything happen to you. If you like, you can stand up in the tub, and I'll just pour the water over you. Will that be alright?"

Maggie considered this in silence then slowly slid off the lounge. "'Fraid," she whispered.

"You can stand up and hold onto the sides with both hands if you like," said Beth. "Can we get you out of your dress and sweater?"

Maggie nodded and began to unbutton the two buttons that were left on the skimpy dress. She hesitated at the edge of the tub. "'Fraid," she whispered again.

Beth offered Maggie her hand, and Maggie

climbed into the calf deep water. She grabbed both sides of the tub and refused to go any farther. Beth wet the wash cloth and soaping it well, began to wash Maggie's thin body. Gradually the grime and greyness that had been on Maggie was transferred to the water. Beth went to scrub her back, and Maggie winced.

'What's the matter, Maggie? Did I hurt you?"

Maggie nodded.

Beth looked more closely at Maggie's back and thighs. There were dark bruises emerging from under the dirt. Beth was horrified. "Who did this to you?"

"Momma."

"Why? Why would she beat you like this?"

"I dropped the egg on the way from the hen house. It was the only one."

Beth shook her head. "We don't beat little girls here, no matter what they do." She shut her lips into a thin line and swallowed back the tears that were very near. She gently sponged off the dirt and inspected the extent of the bruising. "Dear, dear," she said. "Such a terrible punishment over one egg."

"It was all there was," said Maggie. "Are you going to wash my hair too?"

"Yes, and I'll put the pretty yarn in it that Roddy saved for you."

§

Maggie ate supper that night attired in one of Roddy's shirts, her pretty brown hair adorned with the yarn curled around her pale cheeks. She sat very close to Roddy all evening.

James looked at the mantle clock then said, "It's just about time to read and go to bed. We've all had a long day."

"We always read a passage from the Bible in the morning and in the evening," said Roddy to Maggie. "It's a tradition."

James winked at Beth and began to read. Maggie sat and sucked her ever-present thumb, staring at James. When James began their evening prayer, Maggie whispered to Roddy. "Who's he talking to?"

"God, now ssh."

"Does God talk back?"

"Not that I've ever heard Him," whispered Roddy. "Maybe when no one's around, now be quiet."

Devotions were soon over. Beth finished tidying the kitchen. "You children go up to bed now. Roddy, you give Maggie your clean nightshirt to wear until I can make her some nighties."

Once the children had climbed the steep stairs to the bedroom loft, Beth finished her work, then took Maggie's old clothes out to the porch to wash them. She nodded to James to follow her. "The condition of that child was appalling." She poured water into the basin and a little soap then dumped the dress and sweater into the mixture. "These should be burnt not washed, but it's all I have for her until I get a dress or two made for her." Beth began to scrub vigorously. "The bruises on her back and legs were just awful. Awful!" She dumped the dirty water into the waste bucket with a splash and refilled the basin. "People like that shouldn't have children."

James filled his pipe and tested it for draw. "Did she say how it happened?"

"Her mother. I guess she'd sent Maggie to gather eggs. There was only one, and she managed to drop it on the way back to the house."

"Well, they didn't have much so one egg would be precious," said James.

"Not that precious," said Beth. She scrubbed hard at a stain that did not yield. "D'you know she was afraid to get in the tub. She was afraid she might drown."

"You might ask Roddy to find out that story," said James. "Someone may have done something to her, you never know."

Beth emptied the third basin of soapy water and inspected the dress for cleanliness. "That's about as good as it'll get. It'll have to do until I can get something made."

"I noticed you bought some pretty yard goods today."

Beth rinsed the soap out of the garments and emptied the basin for the last time. "I've never made a dress for someone so small before. It'll be by guess."

"Anything'll be better than what she has." James followed Beth back into the kitchen.

Beth shook out the dress and sweater and hung them on the line behind the stove to dry overnight. "Such poverty and there's not any real need for it if her *faither* would only work a little, if what the neighbours say is true."

James tapped out his pipe in the stove. "Well, she doesn't have to worry about that anymore, does she?"

CHAPTER SEVEN

As summer emerged from the coolness of spring, wee Maggie flourished. Her bruises faded, and her thumb was out of her mouth more than it was in. Her thin, small body began to grow and fill out to normal size, and she chattered almost as much as Roddy did.

"Goodness, Maggie, you're growing so fast I'll have to make you some new dresses before the end of summer." Beth looked over Maggie's small stock of dresses. "Some new underwear too, I can see."

Maggie's eyebrows tented into a worried frown, and her thumb took up residence in her mouth, a place it hadn't been much lately.

Beth noticed the expression and the thumb. "Now, Maggie, you don't need to worry, we'll be going to town to get supplies for winter and I can get some more yard goods for a dress or two. I need a couple myself; I seem to be putting on weight too. In the meantime, I think I can let the seams out on these one more time."

The kitchen door rattled."Is anyone at home?" called Robert.

"Aye, we're right here so you don't need to shout," said Beth. "James is getting the big barn ready for haying. I think the fork needed repair. He should be in for tea soon."

Beth gathered up the dresses and folded them for ironing. "What's your news?"

"Elizabeth is busy in the garden today. The beans are nearly ripe for picking."

"My own beans aren't ready yet. Another week I think."

"She's a great gardener," said Robert. "Everything she plants grows, and she has houseplants all winter."

"I see James coming; I'd better get the kettle going." Beth rose and pushed the kettle over the fire box of the stove. It immediately began to bubble.

"Robert, what brings you here?" James extended his hand to his brother.

"I have to go to town tomorrow, and Elizabeth cannot go with me so I wondered whether you'd like to come. I have to have a tooth seen to: it's been bothering me all spring, and I haven't had time to do anything about it. It got to aching last night, and I thought it would never stop. Even oil of cloves didn't help."

James looked at Beth. "Will you mind? You could go over and visit with Elizabeth while I'm gone."

Beth shrugged. "It'll be nice to see Elizabeth. I haven't seen her to visit with her since the spring. The children can play together too."

The visit with Elizabeth was all too brief. At mid-afternoon, Beth called the children together and prepared for home.

"Aw, Beth, do we have to go so soon? We just got here," said Roddy.

Maggie sucked her thumb and looked sad.

"We've been here all day, and I have to make supper for James. He should be home in time for chores."

As they walked toward home and rounded the last bend in the lane, they could see smoke rising from the chimney. "James must be home already," said Beth and quickened her step. She opened the porch door and called, "James, are you home already?"

She opened the kitchen door and the smile disappeared from her lips. "Oh. Poppa." Her tone was flat and unwelcoming. "I thought it was James." She sniffed and then wished she hadn't. The odour was pervasive, and her stomach lurched. She swallowed hard. "What are you doing here, and where are the boys?"

"I left them home."

"That's one question answered. Now, why are you here?"

"I wanted to see my little girl again."

"Hmph," said Beth. "A likely tale."

"It's been eight months." He grinned at her and winked.

"Aye, and it'll be eight months more," said Beth.

"Can't you give your old poppa a cup of tea?"

Beth went into the pantry, keeping a couple of arms length of distance between her and her father. Maybe if I give him his tea, he'll go home and leave me alone, thought Beth. I'd better send the children out to play in case it gets ugly. She carried a plate of bread and the glass of molasses into the kitchen. "Roddy, you and your sister go out to play."

Roddy looked over at Beth.

"Now!" said Beth.

The children scurried out, and Beth waited until she heard the screen door slam. "Have your tea, and then I want you gone before James gets home."

"Now, Bethy, is that very welcoming to your poppa?"

Beth poured tea into a mug and set it down in front of the old man. He grabbed her wrist. "Come now, Beth, I came for some of the good stuff. I saw James and Robert heading in the direction of town this morning and I thought to myself, why should James have all the fun?"

Beth struggled to get out of his grasp.

"That's it, Beth, I've always liked a little struggle for my honey." He grinned and rose from his chair and pushed her against the wall. He began fumbling for her buttons.

A sickening thump and the sound of breaking crockery, and Poppa collapsed in a heap at Beth's feet.

Beth gasped. "Roddy!" She stepped over the unconscious body of the old man. "Whatever …?"

"I didn't like the look of him," said Roddy. "So I waited in the porch and listened to what he was saying."

"But I heard the door close." Beth bent over the limp body of her father.

"I figured you'd be listening for that so I closed it good and loud and stayed inside."

"Thank goodness you did." Beth turned Poppa's head to the side. There was a deep gash running for two inches over his crown. It was bleeding profusely. Poppa moaned. "Hand me that towel," said Beth. "Where's Maggie?"

"I sent her to the hen house to gather the eggs. There'll likely only be one or two, but it'll keep her busy for a few minutes. You know how she is with animals."

"Aye, she'll talk and croon to them for fifteen minutes, and then she'll go and see the kittens and forget all about getting the eggs." Beth pressed the towel to her father's bleeding pate. "Get me another towel. This one's soaked." I hope he doesn't bleed to death in my kitchen, thought Beth. How would I explain that? Poor Roddy too, he'd have to live with that for the rest of his life.

She pressed the second towel onto the wound. The bleeding slowed somewhat, and Poppa began to stir. "Lie still!" Beth showed him no sympathy. "Lie still or you'll start this bleeding again."

Poppa moaned, and for once did what he was told. Beth lifted the towel. The bleeding was down to a faint ooze. "You really laid him open."

"I had to," said Roddy. "I thought he was trying to kill you, and I had to protect you."

"He wouldn't have killed me," said Beth.

"You don't know that," said Roddy. "And anyway, he was hurting you, and I couldn't have that. You're my mother."

Tears sprang to Beth's eyes. "You did right."

"I'm sorry I broke your little churn, said Roddy. He stared with fascination at the blood drying on Poppa's neck.

"It was in a good cause," said Beth. Poppa tried to rise. He began to curse as dizziness struck him.

"Poppa! There are children present," said Beth. "C'mon, Roddy help me get him onto the lounge."

Together she and Roddy hoisted Poppa to his feet and got him situated on the lounge. Beth arranged yet another towel under his head. "Roddy, get me the mop and bucket."

"So that's the *garroch* you've taken in."

"He's a good, obedient boy," said Beth, "He's not a filthy creature as you call him, and I won't have you calling him names."

Poppa moaned. "He had no business breaking things over company's head."

"He did right." Beth gritted her teeth.

Roddy kicked open the kitchen door, dragged the bucket and mop to the stove and began to fill it with water from the tank. "Shall I mop the floor for you, Beth?"

"I want you to guard Poppa while I sweep up the broken crockery, then you can mop the floor."

"Maybe by then James'll be back," said Roddy.

As Beth was clearing up the last of the broken churn, James did return and took in the scene in the kitchen with one glance. "Are you alright, Beth?"

"Yes, thanks to Roddy," said Beth. "I can only imagine what would have happened if he hadn't been here."

"Is that your churn?"

Beth nodded. "What's left of it. Roddy used it as a weapon." She began scrubbing hard at the pool of blood on the floor. "We need a guard dog about the place."

She shuddered. "Take him back home, for I cannot stand the sight of him."

"He's not too injured?"

"I'm not sure I care." Beth gave a bitter chuckle. "The bleeding has stopped. He should be alright."

"What am I going to say when people at church ask me how I got hurt?" Poppa's voice rose into a whine.

"Stay home from church," said Beth. "It never did you any good anyway." She gathered up the mop and bucket and carried them to the porch, slamming the door behind herself.

That evening, Beth and and the children did chores. Roddy and Maggie went to get the cows. Maggie gathered eggs and spread grain for the hens. Roddy cleaned the barn and put down fresh straw while Beth milked. Together Roddy and Maggie carried in wood for the morning. Beth ran the separator and soon had a bucket of milk and a small pail of cream. She lit a lamp and carried them down into the cool darkness of the cellar. As darkness fell, she sent Roddy and Maggie to bed and tried to settle herself to some mending, but it was no use. She rose from the rocking chair and began to pace the short length of the kitchen. I wonder where James is? She took another turn around the kitchen. Och, 'tis not time for him to be back yet. I might as well stop this worrying and do something useful. She sat down in the rocker again and tried to finish the sock she was working on. She stuck her finger with the darning needle. "Ouch!" She heard the sound of running feet, and Roddy arrived in the kitchen in his underwear.

"Are you all right, Mother? I heard you cry out."

"Roddy, what are you doing down here again, and in your underwear? I sent you to bed a half hour ago."

Roddy looked down at his garb. "I couldn't sleep, and when I heard you I thought maybe that man had come back and was trying to hurt you again."

Beth sighed. "Go put some clothes on, and we'll talk about it." I don't know what in the world I'll say to him, she thought as she watched Roddy scramble up the steep stairs to the sleeping loft.

Soon a clothed Roddy rejoined her in the kitchen.

"I'll make you some hot milk," said Beth. "Maybe that'll relax you."

"So was that old man really your father?" Roddy hitched himself onto the lounge and began swinging his feet.

Beth nodded. "Yes, and I wish he wasn't."

"Does he always treat you so?"

"Frequently," said Beth.

"I'd run away from an old coot like that," said Roddy. "He's worse than my father was. At least my Poppa would just take a swipe at us, and if we were quick, we could avoid him. Not that he paid much attention to us anyway. Why didn't you just run away?"

"I did, finally," said Beth. She poured the heated milk into cups for Roddy and herself, then sat down in the rocker again. "How much did you see today?"

"Enough to know that he intended you harm. I could see he was trying to take your blouse off. That's when I hit him."

"D'you know what kind of harm he had in mind?"

Roddy ducked his head as his cheeks reddened. "I t-think so." He stared at the floor as his feet made wider circles in their swing. "It's what Poppa would try with Momma sometimes except he didn't seem to hurt her. Sometimes she'd just push him away, and other times she wouldn't. They'd go upstairs and close the door and warn us kids to stay away." Roddy was silent for a few moments. "Y'know it wouldn't be too long afterwards there'd be a new baby on the way. I don't know if the two things were connected."

Beth smiled at Roddy's description. "That'd be about right."

"Is it the same thing as bulls do to cows to make calves?" asked Roddy.

Beth nodded. "Similar."

"Why would your Poppa want to do that to you? Isn't that wrong?"

"Of course, Roddy. It's very wrong. That sort of thing should be between husband and wife who love each other and not with anyone else."

"But he was going to make you anyway." Roddy's eyes were enormous. "Filthy old scut."

Beth could not hold back the tears. Despite her best effort, they overran her eyes and dribbled down her cheeks and off her chin. She scrubbed at them with the tail of her apron.

Roddy jumped of the lounge and put his skinny little boy arms around Beth's neck. "Mother, don't cry. I'll stay close by and protect you."

"I know you will, Roddy. You're very precious to me." She sniffed and dried her eyes and blew her nose. "Go on up to bed now. I think I just heard James drive in."

Roddy disappeared into the loft just as James came in from the barn. Beth ran to him. He put his arms around her and held her close for a few moments. In a sweater-muffled voice, she asked, "Did you have any trouble getting him home?"

"I had the urge to push him over the bridge when we came to it, and he complained all the way until I finally told him to shut up." James' lips twitched. "I've never spoken to another living soul that way before, but I thoroughly enjoyed it."

She lifted her head. "And did he?"

"He only muttered after that. When I dropped him off at his gate, I told him if he ever came by here again I'd shoot him with rock salt. He stumbled off down the lane cursing and swearing about ungrateful children."

"Humph!" said Beth. "He should be grateful Roddy didn't kill him with the churn. I thought for a minute that he did." James gave Beth a little hug. "C'mon out to the barn. I've got something to show you."

Beth threw her shawl around her shoulders and together they walked hand in hand across the yard. In the night sky, the stars were brilliant, and a half moon was rising. The lantern swung in a small arc by James' side as they walked. He opened the barn door for Beth and led her over to the empty calf pen.

But the calf pen wasn't completely empty. As they approached, the straw rustled, and a whimpering sound came out of the darkness.

Beth drew breath. "A puppy, James?"

James opened the pen door. "Not just a puppy." He pulled back the straw. "A mother and pup."

Beth fell to her knees in the fragrant straw and held out her hand to the puppy. The mother dog growled a quiet warning. Beth withdrew her hand. The mother was a golden colour with a pointed black muzzle; her puppy was similar with a patch of discoloured white around his neck like a necklace. "They're an odd sort of colour. Where did you get them?"

"Robert said they've been hanging around his barns this past week. He trapped them today and locked them into the barn."

"The poor thing looks like she's starving. The pup looks to have fared rather well."

"If you can get close enough to look at her feet, she looks like she's been on the road for quite some time."

"It's kind of late for her to be having pups. I wonder where the rest of the litter is."

"There may not have been any more. I expect she got 'caught' somewhere on her travels. And if there were more, they probably died of starvation. Maybe she ate them to keep herself and the rest of the litter going, and this is the only one to survive."

"How'd you know that Robert had them?"

James leaned on the rail of the calf pen. "I stopped there on my way home after I dropped off your father. I was so angry I had to talk to someone before I hit something. I know that Robert is as safe as a bank."

Beth frowned. "Did you tell him the circumstances?"

"Not in so many words and certainly not the details. He did laugh when I told him that Roddy had broken the churn over his head in your defence. He said, 'Good for him. He's a brave and resourceful little fellow, isn't he.' He also had a few choice words to say about your father and brothers. I don't think your father will be an elder in the church if he has anything to do with it."

Beth's voice took on a worried tone. "He'll be discreet, won't he?"

"I'm certain of it, or I would never have gone to him."

The straw rustled, and the pup stuck his snout out just enough to test the air. "Did you feed them yet?" asked Beth.

"I gave them the meat scraps out of the slop pail for the pigs when I got home. And some fresh milk for the mother when I stripped the cow again. There wasn't much. You must have just finished milking. I figured it's better than they've had for awhile."

Beth rose to her feet. "You're a good man, James. Roddy'll be so excited when he sees them. Maggie too."

"Are you ready for school yet?" Beth asked Roddy.

"I have to brush my teeth," said Roddy. "I still don't see why."

"D'you remember what your mother's teeth were like the last time you saw her?"

Roddy thought for a moment. "Yeah, she only had but two left on the front and they didn't meet."

Beth raised an eyebrow at Roddy. "There's the

reason. You don't want to lose your teeth before you have to. Besides it hurts to have them pulled."

"Papa used to just pull them in the barn. I saved them until they took them from me and burned them."

Beth grimaced in disgust. "Oh, Roddy! Go brush your teeth and be quick about it, I have a surprise for you."

Roddy's eyes grew big and bright. "Oh, boy! A surprise! He headed to the porch to brush his teeth and was back so quickly that Beth doubted he'd done a good job.

"I hope when I check your tooth brush I find it wet," she said.

Roddy sighed. "I did it fast."

"Go get your slate."

Beth waited for Roddy and held the door for him. Together they walked to the barn. Beth opened the barn door. "Are you here, James?" She peered into the gloom and finally saw movement as her eyes adjusted to the light. A forkful of hay dropped from the loft and James hastened down the ladder.

"I thought you'd forgotten," he said and quirked a smile at Beth.

"Absolutely not," said Beth. "I've been on pins and needles all morning not to give it away."

Roddy tugged at Beth's sleeve. "C'mon, Beth, you said there was a surprise."

Beth looked at James and winked. "I guess we'd better show him."

James led the way to the calf pen and opened the gate. A small whimper came from the pile of straw.

"A puppy? You got me a puppy?"

"Sort of," said James. Roddy dropped to his knees and pulled back the straw and saw the mother too. His mouth opened and he sat staring at her for a full minute. Suddenly the mother dog threw herself at him and toppled him onto his back and began licking his face. Roddy ruffled her fur and rolled and tumbled with her. The dog rolled onto her back and let him stroke her stomach.

Beth looked at James. "Well, I guess the dog likes him."

James nodded. "It's almost as if they know each other already."

"It's Pandy," said Roddy. "She came all this way! And by herself, too! And look, she even has a puppy." He held out his hand to the pup who sniffed it and took a tentative lick.

"Who's Pandy?" asked James.

"Pandy was my dog before I ran away. She disappeared the day before I left and I thought she was gone for good and then Papa put the beating on me that evening and I decided I'd had enough so I left the next day. Where'd you ever find her?"

"She found us," said James.

"Actually," said Beth, "she turned up at Robert's yesterday."

"She probably would've turned up here if Robert hadn't trapped her," said James.

"You need to get going for school, now, Roddy. She'll be here when you get home."

"You'll keep her safe?"

"She'll be safe," said Beth. "Is she a good watchdog?"

"The best," said Roddy. "I can't wait to tell the boys." He picked up his slate and raced off across the yard.

"That is a strange story," said Beth. "I wonder how she knew to come here, and how did she find her way?"

James pulled the milking stool next to the cow and sat and settled the milk bucket between his knees. "I dunno. Dogs seem to have a sense that way." He began milking. "I wonder what wee Maggie will do?" The milk soon came in a heavy stream. "The even bigger question is: how did she know to leave home the day before Roddy left?"

"I guess we'll never know," Beth said. "I must get Maggie out of bed so she can see too."

She left the barn and started across the yard. Maggie came running toward her, barefoot and still in her nightgown. "Momma! Momma!" Tears streamed down her face as she hurled herself at Beth's knees. "I thought you were gone." She buried her face in Beth's apron and sobbed.

Beth picked her up and hugged her close. "Why in the world would you think I was gone?"

"I thought the bad man had taken you, and I was so scared."

"*Mo gràdhag*, my little darling, I would never leave you. If I have to go anywhere you'll be right with me."

"But what about the bad man?"

"He will never bother us again." Beth set her lips into a thin, straight line. "Now don't you worry anymore." She set Maggie on her feet and Maggie immediately attached herself to Beth's leg. "C'mon into the barn. I have something to show you." She peeled Maggie off her leg and took her hand. "C'mon, now, Roddy has already seen it."

Maggie let go of Beth's hand and ran toward the barn. She stopped at the sandstone step and stuck her finger in her mouth.

"What's the matter?" Beth pulled Maggie's soggy thumb from her mouth.

"I'm 'fraid of the bad man. He might be in there." She put her thumb back in her mouth.

"He's not," said Beth, "James took him away last night." She opened the door and beckoned Maggie into the warm darkness. "Over here. Now stand very quietly."

Presently the straw rustled and the pup stuck his nose out to test the air. Pandy soon followed.

"Pandy? Pandy!" Maggie was beside herself with joy. She tried to climb over the edge of the calf pen in her eagerness to greet the dog. Beth lifted her into the pen. "Oh, Pandy, how'd you know where to find us?" Maggie flung her arms around the dog's neck. "Look Beth, it's Pandy."

"I know, *mo gràdhag*, my pet. It's a grand surprise."

James came to stand beside Beth. Together they delighted in Maggie's joy as Pandy wagged herself almost in two and licked Maggie's face.

"I must give Pandy some milk." He bent to retrieve the bucket bail to tip a little milk into the battered cat dish. "I'll have to find another basin for her. The cats need their own, especially Momma cat." They watched Pandy lap up the milk as Maggie stroked her back.

"I need to get Maggie dressed and some breakfast into her," said Beth. "C'mon, Maggie. It's time to get washed and dressed and have some breakfast."

"Aw, Beth, do I have to? I don't want to leave Pandy." Maggie's thumb was back in her mouth.

"Pandy'll be here when you get back." Beth lifted Maggie out of the calf pen. "In awhile we'll let Pandy out so she can learn her way around." She set Maggie on the ground. "In the meantime you can think up a good name for the puppy."

§

That evening after the children were in bed, Beth and James rested in the comfortable silence of the kitchen.

Beth broke the silence. "You know, that visit from Poppa really put the fear into Maggie. She thought I'd been taken away by the bad man when I was in the barn this morning."

"So that's what the sniffling and thumb sucking was all about." James rolled onto his side on the lounge and regarded Beth's serious face. "I wondered."

"I don't know how I'm going to ease her mind. In spite of Pandy's reappearance, she's been real clingy. She'd run out to the barn to see Pandy and the puppy and then come running back to see where I was, and her thumb never left her mouth all day except to eat and talk. Tonight she insisted on sleeping with Roddy."

"Maybe she'll grow out of it. After all, she didn't really know why he'd come."

"No, but she knew he meant to hurt me, and she could see what Roddy'd done with the churn."

James sat up on the edge of the lounge. "And you, *mo gaolach*, my darling, how are you?"

Beth shrugged her right shoulder and drew the corner of her lip down into a small grimace. "I'm fine. At least he didn't get to do what he came for." She shuddered. "It has unsettled me, though. I don't feel safe in my own home now."

James reached across and patted her arm that was resting on the arm of the rocker. "It was an opportunity that he took. If he has any sense, he won't do that again. And if Pandy's as good a watchdog as Roddy says she is, you shouldn't have to worry."

"Maybe the pup will grow into a watchdog too. I see it's a male."

"If the children don't make too big a pet of it, it will. If necessary, we can begin locking our doors." James stood up and stretched his broad shoulders.

"I shouldn't have to," said Beth. She followed James' example and stretched too. "I don't know what's wrong with my back these last few months. It's been aching more and more. It seems to be curving more and more too. I can't seem to stand up straight any more." She stretched again and rubbed the small of her back. She stirred the fire and pushed the kettle over the heat. "I'll put down some tea while you check the barns, and we'll have a cup before we read."

CHAPTER EIGHT

That night, wee Maggie woke up screaming. Beth was instantly on her feet, lit the candle and ran to Maggie's bedside. "Whatever is wrong, *mo gràdhag*?" She set the candle on the dresser and gathered the sobbing Maggie into her arms.

"Bad man, bad man was here." She burrowed into Beth's arms as deeply as she could get.

"There's no bad man here," Beth stroked Maggie's tousled hair in an attempt to comfort her. "He's never coming back here. James warned him when he took him home. You just dreamed about him."

"He stinked." Maggie removed her head from the depths of Beth's bosom.

"That he does," said Beth. "He never washes."

Maggie's wild sobbing had diminished to sniffles and the occasional hiccough. "Will I smell like that if I don't wash?"

"That's why you take a bath every week and wash up every day."

"Oh," said Maggie. She thought about this in silence as Beth continued to rock and soothe her. Maggie's eyes began to droop, and Beth laid her gently into bed beside the now alert Roddy and covered her.

"I'll keep you safe," whispered Roddy to Maggie. He put his skinny arm around her middle and was soon drowsing himself.

Beth returned to her own bed and snuggled into the warmth of James' body. "I could kill that old man," she said. "if only it were legal."

"He's a filthy old creature, that's for sure," said James in a whisper. "Is that what the screaming was about?"

"The whole incident has her terrified, and she didn't even see the worst of it." Beth shuddered. "She had a nightmare about it. Only Roddy saw what Poppa intended."

"Did he understand?"

"Well enough. We had a talk about it while you were taking Poppa home last evening."

"I hope Pandy's as much of a watchdog as Roddy says," said James. He cuddled Beth close and was soon sleeping deeply.

Beth lay staring into the pitch darkness. Poor Momma, to have been married for so long to such a beast as him, she thought. How could she have stood it? No wonder she died early. What an evil old man! Her thoughts ran on and on. Perhaps he wasn't like that when he was courting her. Perhaps he was a gentleman, and she thought she was getting a good man. She sighed. I guess that's how it is for women. Once we're married, we must do what we have to do to survive. There's no getting out for us. Where would we go? How would we support ourselves and our children? Thank goodness for James. I wonder when the behavior started? She did say once that he wasn't like that in the beginning. I wonder what changed him? I think she must have known …

Her thoughts went in ever widening circles trying to remember the details of her life when her mother was alive. He never bothered me when Momma was well. It was only after she took sick and couldn't protect me anymore that he really started with me. He tried a few times before that, but Momma always caught him before anything could happen. And I didn't really understand what it was he wanted anyway until I got older. It was the last straw when Samuel tried and I threatened him with the butcher knife. It's a good thing I never told James that part. James stirred in his sleep. Dear James, she thought. She lay for a long time until the room began to lighten with the coming of the new day.

"So, have you thought of a name for the puppy yet?" Beth spooned porridge into bowls for Roddy and Maggie.

"Some," said Roddy. "We thought we might name it after its mother."

"Two Pandys would be one too many." Beth laughed.

"We thought of that, and then I thought about Pandy's full name so we decided to name it Dora."

"What is Pandy's full name?"

"Pandora," said Roddy. "My other mother actually named her. She said she was just like a pest that Pandora let out of her box because Pandy kept coming around every day and begging."

"But Pandy's puppy isn't a girl and Dora's a girl's name," said James from his end of the table.

"Oh," said Roddy. He thought seriously for a moment or two then, "I know, we'll call him Dorn. Is that alright with you, Maggie?"

Maggie sat waiting for her porridge to cool and sucking her thumb. She pulled it out of her mouth to nod and then reinserted it.

"That's a very good name," said Beth. "Now eat up your breakfast and brush your teeth. And you can take the scraps out to Pandy before you go to school."

Maggie's thumb stayed in her mouth for most of the week except when she ate and spoke, and she spoke very little. Beth watched her with serious eyes. Finally, she called Maggie to her side on the lounge and put her arms around her and said, "Maggie, are you still afraid of the bad man?"

Maggie nodded then crawled into Beth's lap.

"Did someone hurt you before?"

Maggie pulled her thumb out. "Don't 'member," and put the thumb back in. She cuddled even closer to Beth.

Beth began rocking and crooning to her. Then she said, "I don't think you have anything to be afraid of, Maggie. James took the bad man a long way from here to his house and told him to never come here again."

Maggie pulled her thumb out. "I sawed him."

Beth stiffened. "When'd you see him?"

"Dunno, yesterday." She shivered and put her thumb back in. For Maggie, yesterday was anything that wasn't today.

"Where, yesterday?"

Her thumb popped wetly out of her mouth. "Chicken coop." She reinserted her thumb.

Beth frowned. "Did he say anything to you?"

Out came her thumb. Maggie nodded.

"What did he say?"

"Took my hand and made me promise not to tell James."

Beth held Maggie closer. "You did right to tell me, though."

"Didn't tell me not to tell you," said Maggie.

"If you see him around here again, you come and tell me right away. Don't talk to him, just come."

Supper dishes were finished, and the Word was read. Maggie still sucked on her wrinkled thumb and stayed near Beth. James took note.

"What's bothering wee Maggie?" he asked.

"I'll tell you about it," said Beth. "We also need to talk to Roddy about what went on at home when Maggie was smaller."

"I see," said James. "It's their bedtime. I'll keep Roddy up a little longer."

In a few minutes, Maggie had gone up to the sleeping loft, and Roddy was perched on the edge of the lounge.

James settled himself into the larger rocker. "Was wee Maggie ever hurt at home that you know of? She seems to be more afraid of the bad man than she should be by now, especially since she didn't see what went on."

Roddy began to swing his right leg in small circles. "Poppa was awful fierce when he'd get into one of his rages."

"Would she see any of that?" asked Beth.

Roddy nodded. "I didn't think she'd remember that far back. She was only tiny then. I think she'd just learned how to walk."

"It was pretty bad, was it?" asked James.

Roddy nodded and stared at the floor remembering. "She got hit that time. He cut her. It was meant for Momma, but wee Maggie got in the way. I grabbed her and ran upstairs and used my hankie to stop the blood. She still has the scar if you know where to look. I stayed close to her after that. I got hit a couple of times myself, but I'm bigger, I could take it. But it frightened her every time."

"Hm," said Beth. "I wonder if that's what has her so frightened by Poppa?"

"I thought she'd forgotten all about it," said Roddy. He yawned. "Can I go to bed now?"

"May I go to bed now," said Beth.

"Are you tired too?" asked Roddy. He hopped off the lounge and grinned at Beth. "May I go to bed now? See, I knew what you meant."

"Of course, you may," said James.

Roddy scampered up the steep steps to the loft. "G'night," he called.

"He is a handful," said Beth. "There's no getting ahead of him."

"But there's no maliciousness in him," said James. He propped his feet on the oven door. "Imagine him, as small as he was, taking care of wee Maggie in that way."

"And him only little himself." Beth picked up her knitting and began to work another cuff for a pair of socks for James. "Wee Maggie told me today that Poppa was here again."

"What?!" James' feet hit the floor with a thump. He sat straight up and stared at Beth. "When?" He rose and began to pace. "Where was Pandy?"

Beth looked up from her knitting. "I don't know. As a matter of fact, that was the one thing I forgot to ask her. As to when, she said yesterday, though that could mean any day this week. The where was out by the chicken coop." Her hands busied themselves again automatically. She continued to look at James. "What're we going to do?"

"I don't know short of talking about him to the elders, and I don't want to do that."

"Notify the constable?" Beth looked down at her work and discovered that she'd dropped a stitch. She sighed and set the knitting aside until she could concentrate.

"Would it bother you if I did?" James calmed himself and sat down in the rocker again. "You know it'd be like telling the community."

"I know," said Beth. "Connie wouldn't do any-thing about it anyway. He's not called Connie for no reason. He's a useless gossip." She smoothed the hem of her apron. "Did you ever hear why he's called Connie?"

"It's short for constable, I do know that. I think it's because he's an old lady when it comes to enforcing the law and the fact that he can't keep quiet about what he does know. I guess we'll have to take care of this ourselves."

Beth tightened her lips into a straight line. "I guess you're right. If we don't, we'll never be safe here. And he'll only get bolder."

The next morning, Beth and James took wee Maggie and walked with Roddy to school before continuing on to Minister MacDonald's house. His charge covered several churches, including Beth's former church. He knew Beth's father well, and from community whispers, had his suspicions, although no proof of wrongdoing. Beth's father appeared to be a pillar of the community.

Minister MacDonald's house sat in the curve of the spruce trees that protected it from the fierce winds that came in off the Atlantic during a Nor'easter. It had sheltered the various ministers over the years and had been built on a little haphazardly as their families increased and filled the existing rooms to capacity. Now the rooms were mostly empty as Minister MacDonald's children had married and moved to homes of their own, either nearby or off-Island.

"D'you know why we're here, Maggie?" asked Beth.

Maggie, who had clung to Beth's hand all the way over, stared up at Beth with frightened eyes and slowly shook her head.

"We're going to tell Mr. MacDonald about the 'bad' man so he can help keep us all safe."

Maggie nodded. Her eyes were enormous.

James rapped on the heavy wooden door. It opened a little, and Mrs. MacDonald stood drying her hands on the tail of her apron and opened the door wider. "Come in, come in." She swung the door wide. "I was just doing a little baking. And who is this?" She peered down at Maggie through flour-dusted spectacles.

"Say hello to Mrs. MacDonald, Maggie."

Maggie popped out the thumb that had taken up residence in her mouth as soon as her mitts had been removed. "'Lo, Mrs. MacDonald." The thumb went back into her mouth.

Mrs. MacDonald looked up at James and Beth. "So this is Little Peter's youngest."

"She's not the youngest anymore. I think by now there must be another one," said Beth.

"She's Roddy's sister."

Beth nodded.

"Will you come in and have a cup with us? I have cookies fresh from the oven. They're still warm, and Himself will be coming out in a minute."

"We actually came to see him on another matter," said James.

"I'll just show you in, then." She turned to lead the way to the study. "He's working on this

Sunday's sermon. He'll be glad of the break. I'll bring tea in shortly."

Mr. MacDonald rose to greet them. "Welcome James. We don't see enough of you and Beth these days." He shook hands with James and indicated chairs for them to sit in. Maggie clung ever more tightly to Beth's skirt.

"What brings you out today?"

"We have a rather serious problem regarding one of the candidates for elder in one of your churches," said James.

Mr. MacDonald leaned back in his chair and frowned. "One of the candidates, you say. And who is that?"

"Beth's *faither*."

"A fine man, but the boys are a little rough," said Mr. MacDonald. "What seems to be the problem?"

"He's not such a fine man as he'd have everyone believe," said James. He recounted the stories that Beth had told him of her life at home. "And now he's coming to the house when he knows I'm not home and trying out his tricks on Beth. He's scaring the children too. Roddy broke the churn over his head to stop him the other day, and Maggie says the 'bad man' has been lurking around the farm, talking to her and telling her not to tell me she'd seen him. She's so frightened she won't sleep alone anymore."

"I see." He was silent for some minutes. "This is,

indeed, serious. You know that I'll have to bring it up with the elders, and he's eager to be one of them."

"I know," said Beth. She hoisted Maggie onto her lap. "He reminded us repeatedly when Momma was alive."

"This must have been what your Momma meant when she asked me to look out for you just before she died." He looked keenly at Beth.

"She did?" Beth's surprise was almost palpable. "She always said we mustn't talk of it to anyone, that it would be a disgrace." She was silent for a moment. "Dear Momma, so she did know. She did her best to look out for me as best she could, even to the end." Beth's eyes filled with tears. "I miss her still. That must have been why she was so insistent that I marry James immediately."

"And why didn't you?" asked Mr. MacDonald.

"As soon as Momma's funeral was over, Poppa put a stop to me ever seeing James again." Beth's tears ran over. "And then began all those years of misery."

Mr. MacDonald shook his head. "I always wondered what happened there. D'you think that Maggie's safe from him?"

Beth pursed her lips and looked at Mr. MacDonald through her tears. "Not for long. He was at me before I even reached maturity. Momma intervened as much as she could, but once she was gone ..." Beth's voice trailed away, and she stared down at her hands. "I want to protect wee Maggie from all that ugliness and evil."

Mr. MacDonald scratched his bearded chin. "Of course, of course." He picked up a pencil and began an aimless drawing on the bottom of his sermon. "What to do, what to do?" He pulled at his earlobe and thought awhile. "I could call a meeting of the elders, I suppose."

"He'd hear about it," said James.

"I guess you're right," said Mr. MacDonald and fell silent for another few moments. "I know what I'll do. I'll talk to David Matheson, and he can talk to the other elders one by one, until they all know about it. We'll swear them to secrecy until we can make some kind of decision."

"I wish I didn't have to do this at all," said Beth. "It was bad enough before, but what'll it be like now?"

"We'll put the fear of exposure into him. One word to the elders' wives, and he won't have any standing in the community at all. And for a man like him, that would be the worst thing that we could do to him."

A gentle rap on the study door announced the arrival of Mrs. MacDonald with a tray of cups and saucers and a pot of tea. She fetched a plate heaped with brown sugar drop cookies warm from the oven smelling of cinnamon and heavy with raisins and walnuts. "Beth, will you pour the tea, please? I'll pass the cookies." Conversation ebbed and flowed in the warmth and comfort of the assembled company. Even wee Maggie seemed to relax. When Mrs. MacDonald's cat wandered into the study, wee Maggie's thumb came out of her mouth, and she sat on the floor and stroked the grey and black pussy and scratched its white bib. Soon it was time to leave, and Maggie's thumb took up its usual place again.

James picked up Maggie and carried her on his shoulders for part of the way home. "I know Minister MacDonald will be discreet in this matter." He took Beth's hand in his calloused one and held it in warmth and communion.

"I hope this is the end of it," said Beth.

"It should be," said James. "Otherwise we'll have no peace."

"If we have to lock our doors, and we're frightened in our own dooryard, we'll become isolated from our neighbours," said Beth. "Maggie's already scared out of her wits, and I'm not all that easy in my own home any more either."

"It's a bad situation," said James. "Especially with the baby coming."

"What?" Beth stopped in her tracks. Suddenly the discomforts of the past two months, the tightening of her dresses and the ache in her back made sense.

James, who had outpaced her when she stopped, returned to her side. He tipped his head at her in question. "You didn't know?"

"I guess I didn't think of that," said Beth. "I thought I was late, but I just thought it was the change coming on a little early. Oh dear, I hope this doesn't mark it in some way."

James put his free arm around Beth's shoulders and drew her to him. "That's only an old wives' tale," he said to the top of her bonnet.

Beth squirmed a little in James' embrace to be able to look up at him. Her eyes were wide with wonder. "I thought I couldn't. I thought I was too old or too hurt or something."

James kissed Beth's cheek, forgetting the presence of wee Maggie on his shoulders. "Apparently not."

Maggie wriggled. "Want to go home," she said. "Bad man might be here."

"Oops," said James and turned them both toward home, his arm still holding Beth close.

Slowly and quietly, word spread from elder to elder. A coolness developed in the community toward Beth's father and brothers. No one was ever rude to them because that was not the way people treated others, but service was exact and to the letter and no more. *Ceilidhs* were no longer open to them, and groups of men dissipated when Poppa or the boys came around. Sermons were preached that pointed directly to that particular sin. Miraculously, the story stayed with the elders for a very long time, although the women eventually figured it out, and they closed rank around Beth too. Nothing was ever said to her, but she felt the warmth and protection of their caring. Dorn grew and became the strong watchdog that Pandy never seemed to be able to. He developed a taste for britches when on alert.

"Have you seen the 'bad man' lately?" Beth asked one day.

Maggie shook her head and continued trying to dress the cat in a sort of cape she'd made with scraps from Beth's sewing basket. "Only once." She looked up from her task and the cat escaped.

"When was that?" Beth watched her carefully from her seat in the rocker.

"Last week."

"Why didn't you tell me?"

"Dorn chased him away." Maggie popped her thumb into her mouth, a place it hadn't been for awhile. "Think he may have bitten him," she said around the thumb.

Beth suppressed a smile. "Good for Dorn. He's a fine watchdog. He'll keep us safe." Beth picked up her sewing again and concentrated on sewing a fine seam on a baby gown she was making. She had put smocking on the yoke earlier and the gown was beginning to look like the one she'd seen in the catalogue. She glanced across at Maggie who had captured the cat again and had succeeded in tying a length of red yarn around its neck for a ribbon. Her thumb was still in her mouth.

"C'mere, Maggie," said Beth.

Maggie rose and came close to Beth who set down her sewing and put her arm around her.

"Climb up here and sit in my lap." When Maggie was comfortable on what was left of Beth's lap from the growing infant within, Beth swabbed off her soggy thumb with the tail of her apron. "You know, *mo gràdhag*, you don't have to be afraid anymore. Dorn and Poppa and Roddy can take care of us."

Maggie nodded and snuggled into Beth's bosom. She folded her hands in her lap the way Roddy had shown her to do. "You need to know how when you go to school because that's how we sit when we're supposed to pay attention," he'd said.

"You know you're going to have a baby sister soon," said Beth. "That's why I'm making all these little shirts." Maggie nodded again, and Beth felt a tear drop onto her hand. She tipped Maggie's face up, and the tears came faster. "Why Maggie, whatever is wrong? Don't you want a little sister?"

"Don't want to go back to Momma and Poppa," she sobbed. "I got hurted. Don't get hurted here."

"Oh, Maggie, you don't have to go back. You're our little girl now. We would never send you back. Whoever told you that you'd have to go back?"

"Roddy. He said that we'd have to be very good and not worry you and James because when the new baby came, you might want to send us back." Maggie sniffed hugely.

Beth pulled her handkerchief from her apron pocket and wiped Maggie's streaming eyes and nose. "Well, he was wrong. We'd never send you back there."

"Never?"

"Never," said Beth. "Now jump down, and let me show you what I've been making."

In the quiet after supper and chores had been completed and Roddy and Maggie were sent to bed, Beth and James sat talking.

"D'you know what Maggie told me today?" Beth's hands automatically picked up her sewing again.

James smiled. "I guess I don't."

"Of course not." Beth laid her sewing down for a moment. "Maggie told me that Roddy thinks we're going to send them back after the baby is born and that they'd have to be extra good to keep that from happening."

"So that's why he's been extra helpful and cooperative," said James. "I wondered why." He frowned. "He asked me if you were going to have a baby just the other day. I told him you were, and he hasn't mentioned it since."

Beth shrugged. "Maggie said he'd told her. How'd he figure it out?"

"He figured it out by observing. After all he does have some experience in these matters with his *maither* having so many. He's very observant, and he usually draws the right conclusions." James looked back to the piece of harness he was mending.

"He's a sharp one alright, and he's growing fast too," said Beth. "I'm soon going to have to make him some new shirts."

"Aye," said James, "and I'll be making shoes again before too long."

"At least we can hand down his old ones to Maggie," said Beth, "She'll be needing new ones soon too."

"We'll have to stuff the toes," said James.

CHAPTER NINE

Over the next few months, Beth sewed and knit and dreamed. It was a peaceful time, and she found herself idling away longer and longer times just sitting. The need to be up and doing seemed far from her thoughts. Every time she started a task, Maggie was at her elbow. "I help, Momma, I help."

"You're a very big help, *mo gràdhag*, my darling." Beth looked down at wee Maggie's darkening curls. "You're not still worrying about us sending you back, are you?"

Maggie looked up at Beth with wide eyes and popped her thumb into her mouth. "Sometimes," she said around her thumb.

Beth leaned down and gave Maggie a hug. "Well, you don't need to be. Nor Roddy either. The new baby will need a big brother and sister so we can't send you back even if we wanted to, and you know we don't want to. Now let's finish our chores and make some cookies for James and

Roddy. You can mix, and I'll measure, and it'll be a nice surprise for them."

Maggie, clad in one of Beth's aprons rolled up at the waist, stirred until the strength of her arms couldn't move the sticky dough.

"Let me help you this time," said Beth. "Shall we put nuts or raisins in them?"

Maggie considered the possibilities seriously for a moment. "Poppa likes nuts and Roddy likes raisins; can we put them both in?"

"Of course, we can, just not quite so many of each." Beth began chopping nuts with the big knife. "You go and rinse the raisins under the pump, Maggie." Beth listened to the irregular strokes of the pump, but there was no sound of water gushing. The sound of wee Maggie screaming and Dorn barking broke into Beth's thoughts. She hurried outdoors to the pump. Maggie stood paralysed with fear, clutching the colander of raisins. Beth scooped her up and sat down on the edge of the steps with Maggie in her lap. "Whatever is wrong?" She wiped at Maggie's tears with the heel of her hand.

Maggie buried her face in Beth's bosom. "Bad man here." Her sobs continued. "He reached for me."

Beth looked around. "He's not here anymore."

"Yes, yes, he is." Maggie's sobs continued in full spate. "He's hiding."

"Where's he hiding?"

"Dunno. Dorn chased him."

"Well, *mo gràdhag*, I don't see him, and if Dorn chased him, he's probably on his way home by now. Let's get these raisins washed and finish making the cookies." Beth set Maggie on her feet and began pumping water. She did not hear the screen door closing quietly over the noise of the pump and the gushing water. They returned to the kitchen.

When they entered the porch, there was a strong odour of unwashed male hanging in the air. Beth stopped in her tracks, turned and herded wee Maggie outdoors. She bent down and spoke to her in a low urgent voice. "Maggie, I want you to run to the back field and tell James that the 'bad man' is in the house. Don't stop on the way. Can you do that?"

Maggie's thumb took up residence in her mouth, and she stood paralysed by the back door. Beth shook her gently. "Maggie! Maggie! This is very important! Run to the back field and get James! Run as fast as you can! Don't stop for anything! D'you understand me?"

Wee Maggie nodded and began to run toward the back lane. Beth watched her until she went over the hill then turned slowly and entered the house.

"Hello, Poppa. I knew you were here."

"And how'd you know that?"

"'Twasn't hard," said Beth and sniffed. "Your odour precedes you. What do you want?"

"I heard I was to be a grandfather, and I came to see if it was true."

Beth shrugged. "It's true."

"When's it to be?"

"In four months time."

"Well, I came just in time then." Her father leered at her. "I always liked your mother best when she was at this stage, round and lush." He stood and reached for Beth's hand.

Beth stepped back a pace and avoided his grasp. "Why don't I make you some coffee first? I can even put a little rum in it for you. I have a little left over from the fruitcake at Christmas."

"That's a very kind thing to do for your old Poppa. It'll be right welcome." He backed up and sat down on the lounge again.

Beth's heart pounded hard, almost to suffocation. I have to stop you once and for all, she thought, otherwise there will be no stopping you. Not with me and not with Maggie or any other daughters James and I might have. She rummaged in the pantry for the coffee pot. She climbed onto the little stool that Maggie had been standing on, to reach the rum on the top shelf of the cupboard. In the back corner, there was a small package that she had forgotten was there. Rat poison! she thought. Do I dare? Will I be caught? Will I go to hell? The last thought had more power over her than all the others. She climbed down and prepared the coffee. She thought of all the ugliness that had been done to her after her mother died and the long years being kept in servitude and at his beck and call, then thought of the consequences to Maggie and other potential girl children. She returned to the kitchen and filled the pot with water from the kettle and set it on the stove to percolate. I can't let this continue. She thought again of the rat poison on the top shelf. Can I do this and never speak of it to anyone, not even James? She felt nausea rise in her throat. I have to, or it will never end. She went back into the pantry and retrieved the packet from the top shelf.

When the coffee was ready she poured a generous mugful and laced it well with rum and rat poison and lots of sugar. She handed it to her father along with a slice of fruitcake, then sat in the rocker and watched him consume both with gusto. "You always did make the best fruitcake, Bethy. It's even better than your mother's." He smacked his lips and licked his fingers. "Any more coffee?"

Beth smiled and took his cup and refilled it with additions. She handed it to him with another generous slice of fruitcake. "I'm glad you're enjoying it, Poppa." She sat and watched him consume the lethal concoction. Her face felt frozen, and her hands were very cold and shaking.

"What's the matter, Bethy?"

"I don't know," said Beth, "I've been having these spells lately. It'll stop shortly." She heard the back door squeak on its hinges and James' footsteps across the porch. "I believe James is home from the back field." She rose and went out to greet him. "Poppa's in the kitchen," she whispered.

James nodded. "Wee Maggie told me he was here. I came as fast as I could."

"Where's Roddy?"

"I left him to mind Maggie out in the hayloft looking for kittens. Did your *faither* say what he wanted?"

"The usual. He didn't succeed. I stalled him with coffee and fruitcake. I used up the last of that rum you gave me for the fruitcake."

"Good for you. And now I'm going to escort him off this farm. He'll have to walk the rest of the way, for I'm not leaving you alone again." He turned and entered the kitchen.

"Finish your coffee, old man, and take the cake with you, you're going home now." James picked up his hunting rifle and checked it for readiness.

Poppa swallowed the last of his coffee in one gulp and stuffed the remaining bit of cake into his mouth. He scurried out the door and headed down the lane as James aimed the rifle at him, then began following him at a smart pace. When he was sure Poppa had left the farm, he returned to the kitchen to find Beth scrubbing at the mug with a wire dishcloth and great energy. She sobbed as she worked. James put his arms around her and held her close. "Why Beth, you're shaking like a leaf. He's gone, and if he has any sense, he won't be back." He took Beth's cold hands in his and began chafing some warmth back into them.

"'Twas lucky the rifle was loaded," said Beth. She clenched her teeth to keep them from chattering.

"It wasn't. I just pretended it was. I'd never leave a loaded rifle in the house or anywhere in reach of children, no matter how reliable the children. Now, why don't you leave off scrubbing that mug and go and lay down. You need a rest after such a hard day. I'll cover you with the quilt and stay here to watch over you, *mo gaolach*."

Beth fell into a heavy sleep laced with dreams of rats and traps and hunting rifles. She tossed and turned and finally awoke with a shrill screech. James was instantly at her side. He held her close and soothed her until the dazed look left her eyes, and her breathing quieted. He rubbed at her wet cheeks with the heel of his calloused hand. "He's long gone, *mo gaolach*. I watched him off the property myself."

"Where're Roddy and Maggie?"

"Still looking for kittens. You haven't been asleep long."

"Are there any?"

James laughed. "No. That's why they're taking so long."

Beth managed a trembling laugh too. "Does Roddy know that?"

"Roddy knew. He just said, 'Yes, Poppa,' and grabbed Maggie by her hand and headed straight for the barn."

Beth struggled out of her welter of blankets. "I must finish the cookies or it will be a waste of good ingredients."

James observed her agitated work in the kitchen with worry in his eyes. He stayed close until Roddy and Maggie returned.

Roddy peeked around the edge of the door and caught James' eye. "Is it alright to come in now? Wee Maggie is anxious to see Momma. I couldn't keep her any longer."

James nodded and Maggie crept cautiously around the door post. "I brought the eggs." She extended the half full basket to Beth. Her eyes were enormous. Beth leaned over and hugged Maggie. "You did the right thing, *mo gràdhag*. It's a little early, but the hens won't know the difference." She set the basket on the pantry counter.

"I'll clean these and take them to the cellar in a moment. Come and sit on my lap." She led the way to the rocker and sat down so that Maggie could climb on. "You're getting to be such a big girl you won't fit on my lap much longer." She put her arms around Maggie and began to rock and sing to her.

Maggie relaxed against Beth and pulled her thumb out of her mouth for a moment. "Will the 'bad man' come back today?" She watched Beth's face intently.

"No. Not ever again. James chased him away with the rifle. He'll never, ever come back."

"Thank goodness for that," said Roddy.

The children stayed close to the house for the next week. Maggie still sucked her thumb and Roddy's young face took on a watchful expression and an uncharacteristic frown line between his eyes. Beth was silent and watchful too. James stayed close to home, neglecting his work in the back field. He observed that Beth ate little and slept restlessly at night. He worried for her and for the baby.

Beth felt her stomach clench every time she thought of her father and what he might have done to her or to Maggie. She knew he wasn't fussy about the age range. Tears came often as she thought of the terrible thing she had done.

I did what needed to be done, she kept reminding herself. She sniffed back another spate of tears. I hope God can forgive me, she thought and sniffed again.

"Beth, what's troubling you so?" asked James. He was sitting by the remains of the supper fire making a pair of shoes for Maggie. The children were outside playing in the last of the sunlight before bedtime.

Beth set down her knitting and looked away. "I'm just so angry and scared all the time. I'm afraid for myself and for Maggie and for our child, if it's a girl. That evil old man!"

James reached over and patted her hand. "He is that."

"I hope he never comes back. In fact, I hope he goes straight to hell. Imagine him wanting to be an elder! Expecting to be one even!" Beth picked up her knitting again. "I hope he goes to the hottest part of hell. It'd be no more than he deserves."

It was a few days before Beth got news of her father's death. The waiting had been unbearable, and it was a relief when the news finally came. Mr. MacDonald came to visit one evening after the children were in bed. Mary came too.

"Welcome," said James. "What brings you out this evening, and Mary too?"

"I have some news for you and Beth. I brought Mary too. I thought she might be of some comfort to Beth at this time."

James face took on a grave expression. "Take a seat. Beth's just upstairs telling the children a bedtime story."

After she had tucked the children in, Beth joined them. Talk was very small and contained little community news. No one smiled.

Finally Mr. MacDonald said, "Beth, I know your father did evil things to you and your *maither*, but for all that he was your *faither*. He's been missing for over a week now. Some of the neighbours searched for him when they could. This afternoon, they found him in the woods by the brook. He'd been dead for a number of days. They think he fainted and fell face down in the brook and drowned. A strange thing though, his trousers were down around his knees as if he'd been short taken."

Beth could not suppress the sigh of relief at the news. She had trouble enough to keep from laughing hysterically.

The funeral was a closed casket and poorly attended. Beth and James went for the look of it. They took Roddy and wee Maggie along so they could see for themselves that the 'bad man' was really gone and no threat to them any more. Beth moved stiffly through the appropriate behaviours around the death and burial. She never smiled. The women gathered around her and took care of her and gossiped among themselves. "She's seriously mourning him after all they say he's done to her," said one. "Aye, but maybe she did care despite the treatment, and it's always sad when someone as bad as he was, leaves this plane and has never repented," said another. "He'll go to the hot place for certain," said a third.

In the days that followed, Beth dropped into a deep depression and sat for long hours empty handed and staring into the distance of her mind. What have I done? she thought repeatedly. She spent long hours trying to pray her guilt away to no avail. She grew pale and thin. James became more and more worried. He took her for a walk one day just to get her out of the house and into the fresh air and sunshine.

"Beth, *mo gràdhag*, whatever is troubling you so? Surely you're not mourning your *faither* still, after all he's done."

"No," said Beth and clamped her lips shut.

"D'you need to talk to Minister MacDonald?"

Beth gasped. "No! Never him!"

"Why not?"

"Because ..."

James shook his head. "Because is not an

answer. If you won't let me help you and you won't let Mr. MacDonald, who can help you?"

Beth began to cry. "No one. God himself can't help me." I can't tell James, she thought, I just can't. "I'm going to go to hell." She sobbed even harder.

James drew her close. "How can you say that? You're one of the best and kindest women I know."

"I can't tell anyone what I've done." She burrowed into the front of his shirt like a child.

James rocked her silently until the sobbing abated somewhat. "Why can't you tell me?" he said to the top of her head.

"You'll hate me as much as God hates me now." Her sobbing increased again. "You'll throw me out, and I would only deserve it."

James held her away from him. "Beth, whatever have you done?"

Beth gulped and took a deep gusty breath. "I thought I could do this terrible thing and keep it to myself, but I can't. If I tell you, you'll make me leave and where will I go? Me and our baby? How'll we survive?"

James gathered her to him. "First of all, Beth, I would never throw you out, no matter what you'd done. But I cannot allow this misery to go on. It's making you sick and if it makes you sick, what is it doing to our baby?"

She watched James' face closely. "I killed Poppa," she whispered. "I thought I could live with the deed, but I can't. So now you know the depth of my sin and my depravity." She stepped out of James' arms.

"Well!" said James. "Well!" He stood staring at her.

"And now you have to bear the weight of it too, if you don't want me to go to the gallows," said Beth and began to shake violently.

James shook his head as if to clear his thoughts. "I don't know what to say." He shook his head again. "That was pretty drastic. Why? When? How?"

"When he came to the house that last time and I sent Maggie to get you, I offered him coffee with some rum and some fruitcake. I was stalling for time until Maggie could get you. I happened upon the bag of rat poison in the back of the cupboard on the top shelf when I went to get the rum from there. At first, I thought of how wrong it would be, even for him, and especially for me and us, so I thought I wouldn't dare. But he had just terrorized Maggie by grabbing her out by the pump. He had started with me at a similar age and gradually progressed until I was old enough. Only Momma could protect me then, and when she died, it got worse. I didn't want that for Maggie or our daughters. So I made the coffee extra strong and added lots of rum and sugar and stirred in the rat poison. He was always so greedy, he wanted seconds of everything, so I did it again. And then you came and chased him off with the rifle. So I had no time to regret what I'd done or to undo it."

James pulled her to him again. "Well, I doubt there was any undoing. I don't know of any anti-dote for arsenic, and it certainly has caused you lots of regret since then."

"I've worried and worried about it all. When there was no word of him all that week, I just thought he'd survived in spite of it. I was a little thankful, but I was scared too. I could only think what he'd do to get revenge on me, or you, or the children. I was terrified."

"I knew he was missing," said James. "I heard the men talking about it at church. Some of them had been called out to search for him."

"And you never told me?"

"You were that distressed over his visit, I didn't want to cause you any more. So I thought it best not to say anything until he turned up. I never thought that you had anything to do with it." He held her silently for a few minutes until her shak-ing subsided. "Funny thing though, Roddy came to me the next day and asked about rat poison and if it could hurt a big person. D'you suppose he figured it out?"

"I hope not," said Beth on the verge of tears again. "I would hate to know that he knew or that I had somehow taught him that murder was alright. Oh, James, what am I going to do?"

"We are not going to do anything, and I'm certainly not going to turn you out for protecting our children and our home. I'm sorry it came to this, for murder is never a good thing."

"Chore time, Roddy," said James. "I'm going to need your help this evening. I need for you to hold Petunia's head while I clean and trim her hooves. Maggie'll have to get the eggs by herself for once."

Together they walked across the yard. Maggie skipped ahead with the basket for eggs.

While they worked James said, "So, did all your questions about rat poison get answered?"

"Yes," said Roddy. "Though I still don't know how much it would take to kill a big person."

"Lots," said James. "At least half a bag of it. Why were you wondering that?"

"I was thinking about ways to get rid of Beth's *faither*, but I didn't know how much to use, so I couldn't. And anyway, when I went to look for it, it was gone."

"A good thing, too," said James. "I used the other half bag this spring by the granary. Some of the rats had survived from the treatment last fall."

"A good thing," said Roddy and stroked Petunia's nose.

CHAPTER TEN

B eth became ever more silent as the weeks passed. Her depression deepened, and she did little by way of keeping house or even keeping herself. Often she wore the same apron for days in a row, and many times her hair hung long in its nighttime braid all day. Roddy spoke of her despondency to James as they did chores one evening.

"Poppa, I'm worried about Momma." His face was starting to take on the seriousness and planes of maturing boyhood.

"So'm I," said James. He continued milking. The peace of the barn and the rhythm of the task did little to alleviate his worry. The hay in the loft rustled with the sounds of pussy stalking mice, and outside the birds were chirping their good nights in the fading light of day. The sweet odour of warm milk overlaid the scent of hay and straw and manure.

"D'you know what's troubling her, Poppa?"

The worry line was back between his eyebrows. "It seems to have begun about the time that her *faither* came. Is it the baby?"

"No, it's not the baby," said James. "And her Poppa is dead and buried."

"What does she have to worry her so, then?" Roddy leaned on his manure fork and watched James' changing expressions.

"I know what she's worried about, but there's nothing I can do for her. Maybe after the baby is born she'll feel better."

Roddy picked up the manure fork and began tossing the excrement out the hatch onto the manure pile behind the barn. "I hope so. Even wee Maggie is worried about her."

James frowned. "Why is wee Maggie worrying about her?"

"She's afraid that Momma will die when the baby is born and that we'll not be able to live here anymore. She said Beth looks all grey and sad, and she never laughs or does things like she used to. Maggie is very frightened. She's still a little afraid that the 'bad man' will come back and hurt them."

"That can never happen. You both were there and saw him being put in the ground. I hope you told her that."

Roddy nodded. "I did, but wee Maggie still dreams of him. She spends a lot of her nights with me when she's had a bad dream."

James looked up from his task. "How often is that?"

Roddy shrugged. "Three or four nights a week. I can hardly get enough sleep myself with her tossing and turning. She's an awful kicker. Besides, we left the grave before it was filled in, and Maggie thinks that someone could have let him out—that he wasn't really dead."

"Oh, dear," said James. He returned to the job of stripping the cow. "I'll have a word with Beth. Maybe she'll know how to reassure her."

That evening after the children were in bed and seemed to be asleep, James pulled his rocker close to Beth's and took her idle hand in his. It was stone cold. He began chafing it to bring some warmth into it. "Beth, can you at least talk about it to me?"

Beth raised her head from the back of the rocker and opened her eyes. "I cannot, for it's no use to talk. I just try to forget all the evil that old man created, even when he was a young man."

"At least we can put the blame where it belongs. If he had not been so evil, none of this would have happened. He brought it on himself."

Beth nodded. "I know that in my head, but it was still wrong of me to do what I did. I had no right to take his life." She began to cry again. "All

I seem to do these days is cry," she sobbed. "I'm glad he cannot hurt us again or anyone else, but why did it have to be me?"

James rose and knelt beside her chair and gathered her into his arms. "Because, *mo gaolach*, you were here protecting your home and family from an intruder with evil intentions. It is the same thing as if I had done it, except I would probably have put a bullet in him for all the harm he's done."

"Would you have?" A fresh spate of tears threatened to overwhelm Beth's control. "That would have been far worse. Who would have looked after us? What would I do with three children and no way to care for us?"

"I know," said James. "They would have had to investigate it as murder, and I would have been hanged."

"And they never think that women can do such things." Beth mopped at her tears with the edge of yesterday's apron. "I guess I'm lucky they think that he had a fainting spell and fell in the brook and drowned when he couldn't help himself."

James nodded and sat back in his chair. "I had a long talk with Roddy this evening while we were doing chores. He tells me that Maggie has been sleeping with him most nights."

Beth looked up. "I didn't know that."

"She's still worried that the 'bad man' will come

back and hurt you two. She's also very scared that you're going to die when you have this baby. Both children are very worried about you, Beth, and so am I."

"I'm sorry, James. It never occurred to me that they'd notice much that was going on with me. Why is Maggie worried that Poppa'll come back? She saw him dead in his casket and put in the ground?"

"Well, they do notice. More than we think, I guess. And Roddy said that the reason that Maggie's so scared that the 'bad man' is coming back is that she didn't see them fill in the grave, and she thinks that someone could have let him out after we'd gone. That he wasn't really dead at all. It's been giving her nightmares."

"Oh, dear-o, the poor child. Half of that would have been enough." Beth sat and pondered the situation for a few minutes. "I think the best thing to do is to take her for a walk to the grave site and talk to her. Maybe after church on Sunday."

The children ran ahead of them as they walked down the narrow road. Beth balanced herself by holding James' elbow. Roddy and Maggie ran ahead. In the trees, the birds chirped their warning calls and then fell silent as they passed. Squirrels picked up the alarm and chirred and scolded from unseen places in the spruces. The ever-present breeze from the sea carried the odours of salt mingled with flowers, grass and evergreens. The Sunday peace penetrated Beth's awareness as it hadn't in a long time.

"I think this is the last time I can go to church until after the baby comes," she said. "I'm getting so awkward and big, and it's only a few more weeks. It wouldn't be seemly to be out in public so close to the birth."

"Of course not," said James. "I can take the children next week, and when the time gets closer, I'll stay home with you. You'll need someone to fetch the midwife when it's time."

"I'm going to take Maggie to the grave today to show her that he really is dead and buried. I think I'll do it before the service so she can sit quietly and let the idea absorb for awhile." The depression of the past months descended again despite the peace of the day. Beth shivered.

"What is it *mo gaolach*?" James took her hand and turned her to look deeply into her eyes.

"Nothing," said Beth. "I had just forgotten for a brief moment about Poppa and his evil, and talking about visiting the grave brought it all back." She bowed her head. "Will I ever be free of this terrible deed?"

James sighed. "I don't know. I hope so because you don't deserve to be burdened with it. You did what you had to do for all our sakes." He drew her into his arms. "When the baby comes, perhaps it will put a barrier in your mind against it."

"Perhaps." Beth pulled away. "We need to keep going on."

Soon they were at the church yard, and friends and neighbours greeted them. "If you'll excuse me for a moment, I have to take Maggie to Poppa's grave so that she can see that he's really there," said Beth. "She's been worrying so."

"Poor wee child, such a thing to be worrying about," said Janet.

"It's just the sort of idea that would set a child fretting," said Elizabeth. "I know mine would."

"You just go and do that," said Mary. "You have plenty of time. I think the boys set up the grave stone just the other day."

Beth located Maggie and took her by the hand. "We're going to look at Poppa's grave." Maggie's hand tightened in Beth's, and she stuck her free thumb into her mouth.

"I think my brothers put up the stone last week. I want to see if it fits properly."

Together they wended their way to the back of the grave yard. Maggie's steps grew slower and more reluctant the closer they got to Poppa's grave.

"For once the boys did a good job," said Beth. "See how tight it fits. That'll keep him from getting out. He won't be able to annoy us ever again."

Maggie's grip on Beth's hand relaxed a little.

"Oh, look, Maggie, even the grass is growing over it. And look there! The buttercups and daisies are starting as well, and there's an ant hill almost built in the middle. He has never been out of the ground so we don't need to be afraid any more."

Maggie pulled her soggy thumb from her mouth. "But maybe someone let him out before the grass grew. They could've, you know."

Beth shook her head. "I don't think so. Someone would've seen them doing that. There were lots of people around that day."

Maggie shivered and stuck her thumb back into her mouth.

"Are you ready to go now?"

Maggie nodded and clung more tightly to Beth's hand.

"You see that he can't get out. The stone's on top of him, and only God can move that stone once it's in place." Beth bent over as far as her pregnancy would allow and hugged Maggie to her. "Now don't you worry anymore, Maggie. It's all been taken care of."

In the final weeks of her lying-in, Beth could not shake the depression. Even the thought of having her own child could not lighten her mood. The brief moment of peace she had felt on her walk to church did not return. Her heart felt like a sack of potatoes in her chest, all lumpy and dirty with this thing she'd done. Even James could not reach her. He waited on her as best he could. But the farm and the animals needed his attention and he had to be gone at least part of the time. Maggie stayed close by, her thumb ever in her mouth. "Can I 'hep,' Momma?" was her constant question.

"No, *mo gradhag*, there's nothing you can do." Beth smiled a little for a moment then lapsed into passivity again. The blackness in her mind did not diminish as hard as she tried to lessen it. Instead it grew and became ever more rock-like. One day, her arms and legs began to itch, and she absently scratched at them. It did not alleviate the itch. Eventually the blood seeped through the cloth of her sleeve, but she didn't notice. James did.

"*Mo gaolach*, what have you done to yourself?" He turned her arms outward and looked at the brown stains on the sleeve of her dress.

Beth looked at them dully. "I don't know. I never saw those before." She lapsed into her habitual silence.

James turned the sleeve up to her elbow. The tracks of the damage were everywhere. Old tracks that were nothing but white scars, newer ones that had scabbed over, and fresh ones, that had been done that day, still seeped with tissue juice. Tears filled his eyes as he looked at his darling Beth. "Oh, Beth, what have you done?"

He looked down once more and saw streaks in the folds of her apron. "Let me see your legs."

Beth listlessly raised her skirts and didn't bother to ask where the children were. Tracks covered her thighs as well.

"What were you thinking, *mo gaolach*?" He pulled her skirt down over her thighs and took her hands again. He sat on his heels looking up at her. He waited for an answer. It was not forthcoming. Indeed, Beth seemed to have forgotten it. "What were you thinking?"

Beth startled at the sound of his voice. "Hm?"

"What were you thinking about when you did this?"

"I don't know anymore. The pain was so intense and itchy, I had to scratch it away, I guess."

"Did it hurt?"

Beth shook her head. "I couldn't feel it, and it didn't help a bit. I'm so tired."

"If I call Mr. MacDonald, will you talk to him?"

Panic filled Beth's heart. "You must not tell anyone, James!"

"I cannot carry this alone anymore, Beth. I don't know what to do for you." James rose from his squat in front of Beth and sat beside her in his rocker. He reached across and took her cold hands in his once again. "*Mo gaolach*, we need you, I need you, and the children need you. And, in a few weeks, our new baby will be needing you even more than we do. This terrible mourning is doing no one any good, especially you. Mr. MacDonald is trustworthy."

Beth sighed. "Do what you must." She closed her eyes. "If he tells, I'll be hanged, and you will be free to find another." The weight in her chest seemed to grow even heavier and she groaned.

James walked the track to Mr. MacDonald's the next morning, oblivious to the sound of bird calls, the breeze sifting through the spruce trees or the late summer scents carried on it. His mind was in such a turmoil that the walk was all too short. Soon enough, he was rapping on the minister's front door. Mrs. MacDonald opened it, wiping her hands on the tail of her apron. As usual, she was flour bedecked and flushed from the heat of the stove.

"James! Come in. I'm just finished setting bread. It seems a never ending task. I made a little extra today for the widow. I heard she hasn't been well, and she hasn't been in church these last two Sabbaths. He's in the study. You know where it is. Just go through." She disappeared in the direction of the kitchen.

James rapped tentatively on the door. It was ajar so he pushed it open.

Mr. MacDonald looked up from his writing. "Oh, James, 'tis you." He rose and held out his hand to James. "Is everything well? You look very worn this morning. Beth ...?"

James shook the minister's offered hand and took the seat indicated. "Beth's not so well, though it's not the baby."

"I see. She should be delivering very soon. We've been expecting word every day."

"I have something very serious to tell you, and it must never go any farther than us. Can I trust you?"

"Hm. It must be very serious indeed." Mr. Mac-Donald listened for the clatter of dishes in the kitchen. All was quiet. He cocked his head. "Let's go for a walk." He rose and buttoned his jacket. "It can be cool on the shore in the morning, should we get that far."

Their walk took them through the woods behind the church. It was peaceful with the chick-a-dee-dee-dee of the chickadees, the caws of the ravens and crows and the distant pecking of a woodpecker still finding his breakfast. In the undergrowth, small animals rustled, going about their daily business, silenced only by the scolding of ever vigilant squirrels alerting everything to the intrusion of humans. The air was sweet with the smell of ferns crushed underfoot and spicy spruce that lined the path. As they walked James related the terrible burden he and Beth had been carrying.

"So she put rat poison in his coffee, did she?" Mr. MacDonald smiled grimly. "Brave girl!"

"Yes, and she thinks she's going to hell for what she did. Or at least to the gallows, if anyone finds out."

"Poor Beth. I've known about the situation since before her mother died, and rat poison was too good for him. He was never like that as a young man."

They walked in silence for a few paces. Then Mr. MacDonald said, "Of course, I'll tell no one, and if anyone's going to hell, it's sure to be her *faither* and not our Beth. It's less than he deserves. I expect his sons will be following him soon if all I hear is true, but that's another story."

"Thank you, Mr. MacDonald. 'Tis a great relief to me to hear that, and I know it will be to Beth too."

"No, as far as this is concerned, he died of drowning and as long as I draw breath no one will ever hear it from me. Would Beth like me to come and see her?"

"She said not," said James. "She didn't want you to know any of this at all."

§

Mr. MacDonald dropped by anyway. The pretext was to ask for James' help in banking the church for winter in a few weeks, but it was not James he wanted to talk to. James was out about the farm as Mr. MacDonald guessed he would be. He rapped on the door and stepped over the threshold. "Are you home, then, James?" He stepped into the kitchen and took in the scene of Beth sitting in the rocker, her head sunk low on her chest and her eyes closed. Her hair hung in lank streels around her ears, and her hands were idle in her lap. There was a greyness about her demeanour that had never been there before. She lifted her head and opened her eyes when he approached her.

"I hear you've been ailing, Beth." He pulled a chair over to sit right in front of her. "I thought I'd come by and see how you are."

"Such terrible pain," she whispered. "If it weren't for James and the children, I would follow him into death. I have done such evil."

"No Beth, not in this instance. You were an instrument of God's wrath. You cleansed the world of a dark evil. There was no repentance in him or his sons. Heaven knows, I tried, but he would have none of it."

Beth's head sank onto her chest again. "D'you suppose he's with Momma now?" She sighed. "Poor Momma."

"I doubt that he is. Our God is a just God. He knows where your Poppa belongs, and He will lock him up and hide the key."

A tiny laugh escaped from Beth. It was the first time in months, and it felt strange. "I hope it's as warm as they say, for I fear I shall be joining him when my time comes."

"Never say that again, Beth." Mr. MacDonald cleared his throat. In First John 5:18, it says: 'We know that whosoever is born of God sinneth not; but he that is begotten of God keepeth himself, and that wicked one toucheth him not.'

"You are a child of God. I have known that since you were born. I baptized you, and I have watched you grow and become the fine woman that you are. You are here for a purpose, and you are fulfilling that purpose every day against some very great difficulties. Do not worry any more about evil and being condemned by God. He sent you for this purpose because he knew you had strength. Your *faither*'s evil toward you just made you stronger, and you did what you needed to do to protect your children and James. Think what would have become of them if you hadn't stopped him. Think what would have happened to James if he had done the necessary deed. Then where would you and the children be? So even if it was against the commandment to not kill, it was to God's purpose. He never hesitated to kill where necessary. This is not something I would preach so don't repeat it, but I've thought it a long time. Now, I want you to stop worrying and to take up your duties as wife and mother again. You have a baby coming that will need all your wisdom and care, as do Maggie and Roddy. The action will always be with you, but it will shrink until it becomes a tiny, shrivelled pea in your memory."

"May I tell James what you said?"

"Of course, a husband and wife should always be open with one another, and I know that James is safe. Now, I must go. Greet James for me. I will pray for a safe journey through childbirth for you."

Beth sat for the rest of the afternoon, pondering the things that Mr. MacDonald had said. Perhaps I did do God a service, she thought. Maybe even the world. Certainly this household. Her mood slowly lightened. She sighed. I still don't know why it had to be me, she thought. Why couldn't he just have fallen out of the hay loft and broken his neck? She looked down at her dress and apron and could not call to mind when she had last changed them. I'm a disgrace, she thought. What must James be thinking? He deserves better than this. She carried a jug of hot water upstairs and poured it into the wash basin. I can at least wash my face and put on clean clothes.

When James came in from the fields at supper time, he found a somewhat transformed Beth. She was cleaner and neater than she'd been for a long time, and a nourishing meal was on the table. He watched her work around the kitchen and saw that some of the briskness had returned to her activities, and her face did not seem so downcast as before although there was still a sadness in her eyes.

After the chores were finished and the children had been in bed long enough to be reasonably sure they were asleep, James pulled his rocking chair closer to Beth's and took her hand in his calloused one. For a change her hand was not cold. He looked into her eyes, and the old Beth looked back. The sadness still lurked there, but she smiled at him.

"So, are you feeling better, *mo gaolach*?"

Beth nodded. "Not cheerful exactly but the blackness seems to have lifted a little. Mr. Mac-Donald was here this afternoon and we talked for a long time. He quoted me a verse of scripture that made sense. He also said that I was actually an instrument of God."

"It's him who would know. I think, over the years, he's seen every evil this community can produce and a lot of the just plain foolishness."

"What I did was evil and against God's

commandments, but it doesn't seem so awful anymore. He said I had a duty to you and the children and that I was protecting you. I suppose I'll always carry this in my heart, but at least I will be able to carry it now."

"He's a good man," said James.

CHAPTER ELEVEN

In the next few weeks, Beth did her best to appear cheerful. The heaviness was still in her heart, but it didn't seem so weighty now. The scratches slowly healed on her arms and legs, and when she found her thoughts wandering to what she had done, she firmly pulled them back to concentrate on whatever task she was currently occupied with. She talked more to the baby as if it had already arrived. Her voice seemed to quiet it, and it seemed to be sleeping more. At least that's what Beth imagined. I wonder if they do sleep inside like that, she wondered. She imagined the baby all nestled and curled in the warmth and darkness of her belly and smiled at the idea. "I guess after all my distress you need the rest," she said aloud. "So rest up, little one, we have a big job ahead of us."

When the baby was quiet for several days, Beth began to worry. Her back ached more, and it was getting harder to sleep at night. There was no one nearby to ask. I hope I haven't done you irreparable harm, little one, she thought, then began to worry some more. I wish Momma was here. She'd know. Beth lay down on the lounge to rest her aching back, but it did no good. She rolled off the lounge to a great gush of water between her legs. Oh, dear, what am I going to do? I can't even hold my water now. She looked down at the puddle at her feet. The water still dribbled down her legs. The ache in her back intensified until she gasped for breath.

"Maggie, run and get James. He and Roddy are in the big barn. Hurry now. I need him immediately."

For once, Maggie didn't dawdle and daydream. In a minute or so, James was in the kitchen with Beth. "Is it time, then?"

Beth nodded. "Tell Roddy to take Maggie to Robert's house and to stay there himself until you come for him. You need to go for the midwife. I don't know how long babies take to get here once they decide to come."

"You'll be alright by yourself?"

"I have to be, don't I?"

James nodded. "I'll be as quick as I can."

In a moment, she could see him running across the hill field toward Megan's house. The children dawdled their way across the home field in the direction of Robert's. Another contraction took her attention, and her world closed down to the task at hand. She paced the tiny kitchen, avoiding the wet spot on the floor. I need to wipe that up, she thought absently every time she passed it. Water still trickled with each contraction, and she rolled a towel and put it between her legs. Oh, James, do hurry, she thought as another contraction came on. She gasped with the intensity. I didn't know how much work this would be. Why did no one ever tell me? She continued to pace.

In awhile, James came back with Megan who bustled about the kitchen organizing things for the birth. James hung helplessly about, not at all sure if he was to go or stay.

"Go and get a mop and clean that up," commanded Megan, to give him something to do and keep him out from underfoot. Beth continued to pace.

"Beth, I want you to lay down. I need to see if you are anywhere near delivery. James, you need to leave now."

James looked at Beth with distress in his eyes. "Can I come back when you're finished?"

"If you don't get in the way." Megan rolled up her sleeves and washed her hands. "Now, shoo."

"I won't be far," said James. He went outdoors and sat down on the steps. The sun was warm on his back, and he thought of how many women gave birth every day and how few of them died from it. But still, it was his Beth going through it now. He groaned. And I did it to her, he thought. He thought of all the anguish she had gone through that summer on account of her father, and his heart ached for her. That evil old man, he thought. All her life. He deserved everything he got. Beth did not deserve a *faither* like him. I hope she doesn't have to pay any further for it. God, let this all end safely and well, he cried in his heart.

Beth paced the kitchen most of the afternoon. The birth pangs came ever closer together. Finally, nausea overcame her, and the need to push came too urgently to be ignored. "I think it's time," she gasped after the latest contraction.

"You need to lay down and let me see," said Megan. "Don't worry, I've padded the lounge well. It will be easier to deliver there than in bed. The bed's too soft."

Beth lay down, and her legs opened wide on their own as if to make room for the impending birth. At the next contraction, a tuft of dark hair appeared and then retreated. "You're almost ready," said Megan. "In a few minutes, this'll all be over."

Another contraction hit Beth full force. She groaned loudly.

"Good," said Megan. "The head is right down. Another few pains should see it here."

The contractions gained strength. They came in close succession with only enough time to barely recover between them.

"At the next one, I want you to push with all your might and don't stop pushing until the pain dies down."

Beth took a deep breath at the start of the next contraction, and near the height of it, began to push hard. Her back curled up with the effort. She felt something give below. I hope I haven't broken anything, she thought idly, not really caring whether she had.

"The head is out," Megan announced. She eased the shoulder around. "One or two more good pushes like that should see it born."

"Good," said Beth through gritted teeth as the next contraction took hold. She gathered her strength and her breath and pushed again. She felt the baby slide out. Thank God, she thought.

"It's a girl," said Megan. She let the pulsing in the cord stop before severing it. She held the baby by her heels and stroked her back, and she uttered a choking cry and then another lustier one to announce her arrival. Megan wiped her face then wrapped her in warm towels and handed her to Beth. "Just one more push, and it'll be all over. You might want to put her to breast to speed the process."

Beth looked up in alarm. "Another one?"

Megan nodded. "You haven't delivered the afterbirth yet."

"Oh, dear," said Beth as the last contraction took over.

"I'll just clean you up, and then James can come in and see his baby girl."

James stood staring down at his wife and his baby girl, and wonder and love filled his heart for the both of them. Their beauty in that moment was almost too much to bear.

Beth blushed under the intensity of his gaze. "D'you want to hold her?" she asked.

"I just want to look for a moment." He sat down by the side of the bed. "She's so tiny. I don't think I've ever seen a newborn before. I was one of the younger ones so I was hardly aware when the last two were born. The only real newborns I've seen are calves."

Beth laughed. "Oh, James, she's not a calf."

"I know that. I only meant …"

"I know." Beth reached over with her free hand and patted his arm. "I've never seen a real newborn either. I was the youngest, and, of course, none of the ladies came out of their lying-in for nearly a month after the birth, so the smallest ones I've ever seen were already a month old." She looked down at the baby sleeping in her arms for a moment. "What are we going to name her?"

James looked bewildered. "I don't know. We

haven't even thought of that. I don't know babies' names."

"I was thinking of Laura. My mother's name was Laura." The baby stirred in Beth's arms and opened her eyes to look straight at her, then seemed to almost smile. "I guess she likes that name. What'll we give her for a second name?"

James thought for a moment. "Jean? It was my grandmother's, and I've always liked that name."

"I think it means 'precious gift from God.' Caroline and I were talking about names once, and she had a book of baby names. I don't know where she got it from. That's Caroline's second name, too."

"Laura Jean. That's nice." James smiled down at them. "Shall we have a cup of tea on that, and then I'll go and get the children. They'll be anxious to see their new sister."

An hour later, Beth stirred from her nap to the sound of Roddy and Maggie's return and James admonishing them to be very quiet that the baby was sleeping. She smiled at the homeyness of the sound. "It's fine, James," she called from the bedroom loft. "Laura's awake just now. Are their hands clean so they can hold her?"

"Go wash your hands," she heard James say. "I'd better wash mine too."

"You mean we can hold her?" said Maggie. Her little girl's voice piped up the steep steps. "Isn't she really tiny? We might break her."

Beth could hear James laugh. "I don't think there's any fear of breaking her, but we do have to be gentle and clean. Let me see your hands, Roddy." There was silence from below. "Go wash again. Use new water. Maggie? You, too." A scurry of activity began, followed by splashing. Then, "Let me see." Quiet again while James inspected hands. "Alright, you can go up now, but be quiet. Beth's tired." A rush for the stairs, then the sound of feet tiptoeing across the rough floor boards of the loft. Maggie peeped around the door frame.

"It's fine, Maggie, you can come in." Beth turned on her side and cradled Laura in her arm. "See?"

"Ooh," breathed Maggie. "She's beautiful." She reached out and carefully touched Laura's hand. "She's so soft." Maggie pulled her hand back and put it behind herself.

Roddy just stood and stared.

"What do you think, Roddy?" said James.

"Dunno," said Roddy. "She's pinker than Momma's babies. They were all red and wrinkled. She's bigger, too." He stared for a moment longer, then nodded. "She's pretty. She'll do."

"D'you want to hold her?" said Beth.

"Can we?" asked Maggie.

"Of course," said Beth. "Here, James, you take

her and hold her while I go to the outhouse. I'll only be a moment."

James' eyes widened in alarm. "I've never held a baby before."

"It's easy." Beth rolled to a sitting position on the edge of the bed. "You do it like this." She demonstrated. "Just be sure you support her head and back on your arm." She handed the baby to James. Laura opened her eyes wider and looked up at James then nestled into the crook of his arm with that odd little ghost of a 'smile' she had produced earlier.

"Ooh, look," said Maggie. "She's smiling."

"I don't think so," said Beth. She wrapped herself in her shawl. "Newborns don't know how to smile until much later. At least I've never heard that they do. They say it's just gas."

"I doubt it's gas already," said James. "She's hardly had time."

Beth laughed. "You just want to believe she's smiling."

The next days were filled with learning to take care of Laura Jean. Beth's milk came in, painfully at first but was much relieved when she nursed. She became adept at changing diapers, and she and Maggie always seemed to be at the wash tub scrubbing baby things.

"You're such a help to me, Maggie. What will I do without you when you go to school next year?" Beth reached out and stroked Maggie's tousled hair as Maggie folded another diaper haphazardly.

Maggie frowned. "I be six then. I be a big girl then."

"You certainly will," said Beth. "You're already my big girl. It'll soon be time to teach you your beginning numbers and letters. Would you like that?"

Maggie ducked her head. "Roddy already showed me."

"He did? When was that?"

"In the summer."

"Where? I never saw you making letters."

"In the sand by the hen house. He made me do them every day."

"Can you still do them?"

"Of course," said Maggie, her voice tinged with five year old scorn. "I can say them too. Want me to say them, Momma?"

"I'll be very happy to hear you say them."

"A-B-C-D …," Maggie began the singing chant of the alphabet. It was a recognizable approximation to the tune. "X-Y-Zed. Now I've said my A-B-C's, tell me what you think of me." She grinned up at Beth.

"That is excellent, Maggie. You'll have to sing them again for Poppa when he comes in for supper." Beth rose and laid Laura Jean in her basket. "I must do a little baking; there's not a morsel for a mouse in the pantry. Will you look after Laura Jean for me while I make a pudding for supper?"

Maggie took up her post beside the basket and played quietly with her doll. She hummed the ABC's to herself, and Laura Jean watched her with big blue eyes and the strange little 'smile' she wore when something pleased her.

Beth finished beating the cake, put it in a pan, then popped it into the oven and stoked up the fire a little. "There, that should be done and cooled in time for supper." She sat down in the rocker and sighed contentedly. This is the happiest I've been in a very long time, she thought. Maybe ever. The thoughts of what she had done still lurked just under the surface. She sighed again. Will I ever be free of this? She wondered and then pushed the thought back to its hiding place in her mind.

"Are you sad again, Momma?"

"A little," said Beth. "Having a baby is a big responsibility."

"What's 'sponsibility?"

"D'you remember when we talked about the word duty the other day?"

Maggie nodded. "Uh huh. It means to do what's right and not fail."

"Good for you," said Beth. "Well, responsibility means the same thing. It's just a bigger word for it."

"Oh," said Maggie, then sat quietly thinking about it for a moment. "If I learn enough big words then maybe I can stay home and he'p you more."

Beth laughed. "It doesn't work like that, and anyway don't you want to go to school with Roddy?"

Maggie shrugged and popped her thumb into her mouth. The habit had been absent since shortly after their visit to Beth's *faither*'s grave.

"Maggie? When someone speaks to you, it's polite to answer them."

Maggie nodded.

"Are you afraid to go to school?"

"Yes," said Maggie.

"Why?"

"Bad man might be there."

"Maggie, the bad man can't go there any more than he can come here again. I took you to see his grave. Don't you remember?"

Maggie nodded again. I 'member. But maybe he's not there anymore. Maybe he got out."

Beth sighed. "Didn't I show you the heavy stone the boys put over him?"

Maggie nodded once more. "But I sawed him."

"Where?" Beth's alarm bells went off in her mind. "When?"

"Yesterday, by the chicken coop. I writed my letters in the sand, and he comed and talked to me."

"It must have been a different man," said Beth. "It must have been just someone who looked like him."

Maggie started to cry. "It was, it was. I sawed him."

"It's alright, Maggie. Hush now, you'll be waking Laura Jean. I can go back to church on Sunday, and I'll take you up and show you the grave with the big stone again. You can see for yourself and know for sure. Will that be enough?"

Maggie's sobs lessened to a sniffle. "I s'pose so." Her thumb remained in her mouth.

Beth rose to test the cake. It was done so she set it in the pantry on the window ledge to cool. Her mind ran riot on what Maggie had just said. I need to talk to James about this, she thought. The only one I can think of who would look enough like Poppa to be mistaken for him by Maggie is Samuel. I don't want him around here either. He was almost as bad as Poppa. The fear was back in her heart. I need to keep my children safe, she thought.

It was later that evening before Beth told James about Samuel's possible visit with Maggie.

"What does he want here?" Concern roughened

James' voice. "We cannot have him roaming freely about the farm. Are you sure it was him?"

"He's so like Poppa I can't imagine who else it could be." Fear and worry clouded Beth's expression. "I don't know what we can do. I cannot do again what I did to Poppa, and I cannot live with the worry of that and Samuel too. He's as bad as Poppa."

"We need to live safely on our own farm and raise our children without fear of molestation." James pulled his feet off the oven door where he'd been warming them. They hit the floor with a thump. "I'll fill his backside with rock salt if I have to. He will not continue to lurk around this farm."

"Maybe Dorn can help you deal with him." Beth managed a wobbly giggle at the idea. "He's turned into quite a watchdog."

"He's still just a pup," said James, "and I'll have to catch Samuel hanging around first. Keep Maggie close by until I do."

There was not long to wait. For the next few days, James worked around the barns, his hunting rifle primed with rock salt and near to hand. I'm not going to wait for any conversation with him on this, he thought.

Maggie dawdled around the farm yard as was her habit, playing with the kittens and talking to the hens. She carried her basket with her and spent time watching the ants build an ant hill at the roots of the maple tree that had grown voluntarily by the back fence.

"Hello, Maggie." Samuel smiled behind his beard, baring his yellow, crooked teeth.

Maggie screamed and dropped her basket but stood frozen in fear.

Samuel reached out his hand to take hers. Maggie backed away and stuck her thumb into her mouth, all the while watching Samuel as if watching a snake.

"G'day, Samuel." James stood behind Samuel with his rifle cradled in his arms and Dorn at his side. "What have you done to frighten our Maggie?"

Maggie ran to James and grabbed onto his thigh. "Bad man, bad man," she said around her soggy thumb.

"I can see that," said James. He reached down and patted her shoulder. "You're safe with me." He moved a step closer to Samuel. "What makes you think you can come to my home and scare my daughters and my wife?"

"I was just paying a visit." Samuel eyed the rifle warily. "Just a visit to Bethy. She's my family after all," he whined.

"You're not welcome here," said James. He took aim at Samuel's anatomy. "Go and don't come back." Dorn growled. Maggie shrank behind James' legs. "Run to the house and stay with Beth, Maggie."

When Beth heard the sound of the rifle and Dorn barking and growling at the barn, she looked out the window and saw a flash of darkness disappear into the woods. James must be shooting rats, she thought, then frowned. I wonder where pussy is, and why is Dorn barking like that? The screen door slammed, and Maggie hurled herself at Beth and buried her face in her lap. "Bad man," she sobbed, "bad man."

At last, James came in and hung his rifle in its accustomed place. "He won't be coming back. He's probably halfway to the shore by now. I didn't know any man could run that fast."

"What'd you do to him?" asked Beth. She glanced down at Maggie who still clung to Beth's aproned leg and sucked her thumb. "Nothing permanent I hope." She kept her arm around Maggie's shoulders and held her close.

"No." James held his hands out to the lingering warmth of the breakfast fire. They were shaking. "Though he won't soon forget."

Beth took his hands in hers. "And Dorn?"

James managed to chuckle. "Dorn had fresh meat for dinner."

"Oh, dear," said Beth. She sat down in the rocker and took Maggie onto her lap. "I hope he didn't sicken himself."

"It wasn't enough, but it will leave a scar."

Beth turned to Maggie. "There, you see Maggie, Poppa and Dorn took care of the bad man once and for all. He won't be coming around here any more. D'you understand?"

Maggie nodded slowly. "I knowed they let him out when no one was looking."

Beth blinked. "Oh, no, Maggie, there were two bad men. One we buried, and his son who looks just like him who's still alive. That's the one who was here today. D'you see now?"

Maggie nodded again and pulled her thumb out of her mouth. "I think so. Your Poppa was one bad man, and he's buried. And this one just looks like him?"

"That's right. And your Poppa made sure he won't want to come back here. He knows what he'll get if he does."

The porch door banged, and Roddy came in wiping his forehead on the sleeve of his shirt. "He's gone. I followed him almost all the way to Uigg. He never stopped running." Roddy chuckled. "I don't think he knew I was following him, but he kept looking behind and moaning. You got him fair and square. He'll not be able to sit for a week."

"We need to talk about this," said James. Beth nodded her agreement. "Sit down."

Beth reached over from her seat in the rocker and pushed the kettle closer to the fire. "I'll just make some tea. A wee *strupach* won't come amiss after your hard work."

Roddy found a seat on the end of the lounge. "Yes, sir?" It was the first time Roddy had ever called James sir.

James cleared his throat. "You're old enough to know now that violence is an extreme reaction to any situation."

Roddy nodded.

"D'you know why Samuel was hanging around?"

"I think so," said Roddy. "The same reason that Beth's Poppa was, only Samuel wanted Maggie instead."

James nodded. "And you know why that's wrong. But people as bad as Samuel and Beth's Poppa have to be stopped, and sometimes you have to take extreme measures to stop them. I don't condone violence, and it grieves me to have to act violently toward any human being. I will carry the distress of this 'til the day I die." James bowed his head.

"You were protecting you home, James." Beth rose to put down the tea. Maggie followed her into the pantry. Beth set out mugs, a plate of biscuits and the molasses. "You have a right to protect your home." She set the table with appropriate cutlery. "Run to the cellar, and get me the milk and the butter, Maggie. There's no bad man here now."

In the days that followed, Maggie became less clingy and Beth began to relax a little. Laura Jean nursed better, and peace seemed to be restored to the household. James kept his distress well hidden.

"I'm going over to Minister MacDonald's," he said. "Will you be alright by yourself for an hour or so?"

A shadow of worry crossed Beth's face and was quickly gone. "I guess so, but don't be too long. I'm still not really settled even though we haven't seen or heard anything since he was here."

"I know," said James. "You do a good job of hiding things, but I can tell by how watchful you are. I won't be any longer than I have to."

James' trek through the peace of the woods did little to ease his spirit. At last he arrived at Minister MacDonald's and knocked on the door and stepped into the dimness of the back porch. His eyes took a moment to adjust to the light, but the faint odour of the lye soap by the wash tub and the richer odour of the slop bucket for the pigs gave him no doubt of his location. He knocked on the kitchen door. Mr. MacDonald opened it.

"James! Do come in. What brings you here today? Nothing wrong, I hope."

James stepped into the kitchen still warm from the mid-day meal. "I have a serious matter to discuss with you."

"Come into the study." Mr. MacDonald turned to lead the way. "Not Beth, I hope." He ushered James into the book-cased room. "Have a seat, then."

"No, not Beth or the children." James hesitated. "Well, not directly." He paused and sat down, then frowned. "Samuel has been lurking about the farm lately. He's been lying in wait for Maggie and trying to make friends with her."

"Has he succeeded?" Mr. MacDonald leaned back and tented his fingers.

James shook his head. "No, Maggie's afraid of him. She thought he was Beth's *faither* come back from the dead. She calls him the 'bad man.'"

"Oh, dear, that would be a fright. What did you do?"

"I caught him the second time and filled his backside with rock salt and set the dog on him."

"I see." Mr. MacDonald pursed his lips. "So that's why he was standing when I was at the store the other day. John Two offered him an empty nail keg to sit on, but he refused. He seemed a little anxious too. He kept looking around and checking the door every time it opened." He nodded thoughtfully. "Is there something you want me to do about it?"

"I don't know," said James. He shifted uneasily in his seat. "I truly don't. I don't like being violent with another human being, and I'm afraid of what it's teaching the children. But I cannot have that kind of thing going on in my own home."

"Of, course not." He thought for a moment. "I can alert the other elders.

"Beth won't like it, and you know how word travels around here."

"Maybe that's a good thing in this instance. The more people who know, the less likely he'll be to pay any more visits."

James sighed. "It's a terrible thing how evil begets evil. I sometimes wonder how someone as wonderful as Beth could come out of such a family."

"She's her mother's daughter." Mr. MacDonald sat and thought back to Beth's mother. "There never was a kinder, gentler person in this community. It was a real loss when she died." He sat in silence for a few minutes. "By the way, how did John become John Two?"

"He took over from his father, John the Store, when he came of age and married. Of course, he was John Two before that whenever anyone wanted to distinguish them, but you didn't hear it as much."

"I've always wondered that. He was already half grown when I came here so I didn't hear the beginning, and I've never thought to ask."

James rose. "I won't take any more of your time."

"So you can accept the oversight of the elders?"

James nodded. "If I must. They're good men and their wives, should they find out, will be sympathetic to my Beth."

CHAPTER TWELVE

The days passed uneventfully. There was no sign of Samuel or of any of the other brothers. They did not even come to church. Eventually the atmosphere in the community changed subtly as the women came to find out the parts of the story they were given to know. There was never a word said directly to Beth or Maggie, but the women rallied around them protectively in one way or another. The men turned their shoulders away from the brothers whenever they came near. Service in the shops was much less accommodating toward them. They found that they had to make the long trip to Charlottetown more and more often for things that John Two was currently out of and wouldn't be getting any more of until the spring. In truth, his store room was filled to overflowing for the autumn.

"Imagine the brass of that fellow," said Sadie. Her knitting needles clicked faster and harder at the thought of what might have been.

"It's difficult to believe that Laura could have had such a brood," said Mary.

She peered near-sightedly at the darning needle she was trying to thread. "She was such a good, kind person."

"Aye, she was a God-fearing woman indeed," said Cassie. "A true saint if ever there was one." Her rocking chair gained speed. "I heard that the boys were going to go west for the harvest this year."

"They should stay there if they have any sense," said Sadie, "for they're no longer welcome here even though they are one of our own." Her hands flew over the stitches. "It's a terrible thing to go after a good woman like that, but to go after a child who doesn't know and is too little to defend herself." Her voice took on tones of anger. "Och, I dropped a stitch." She laid her knitting in her lap and leaned back and sighed. "No woman is safe as long as they're around."

"Oh, aye," said Cassie with a hint of laughter in her voice. "And it's certain your man's new sock isn't safe either if you drop your stitches."

Over the summer, Maggie relaxed a little, but the air of watchfulness was still about her even into the fall. Her thumb was less in her mouth, and she lost her baby talk in time for school.

"We'll have to make you some new dresses for going to school. Two, I think," said Beth.

Maggie's eyes grew round. "Two new dresses?"

"I think so," said Beth. "One to wash and one to wear. We'll go to John's and pick out something pretty tomorrow." Beth stirred flour into the drippings from the roast. It began to thicken immediately. "Supper's almost ready now. Go and call Poppa and Roddy to wash up then come and help me set the table."

Soon they were all seated around the table and the blessing was asked. "Start the meat, then, James, and I'll pass the potatoes. You're looking very tired this evening."

"Aye. Roddy and I have started clearing the orchard out. The little trees from the woods were encroaching, and they were in danger of taking over the apple trees. I thought it best to start clearing the bigger ones. I've been putting it off all summer, but it has to be done before they get any bigger or I'll never get them out. As it is, they're already stubbornly rooted."

"We made good headway, though," said Roddy. "It's good we do it now before school starts. I won't be able to help you then." His brow furrowed, but the expression was quickly gone.

But Beth noticed. "What is it, Roddy? You look worried."

Roddy shrugged one shoulder. "Nuthin'."

Beth and James exchanged glances.

Roddy sighed. "I've been thinking a lot lately about school. In another year, I'll have gone as far as I can here in the little school. What then?"

James sat back in his chair and pursed his lips, then said, "What do you want to do? You can always come home and work with me. There's enough work for two around here. Or were you thinking of something grander?"

Roddy shrugged one shoulder again. "I dunno. I was sort of thinking that I'd like to study more. Now that I've learned to read, I was thinking that I'd like to go farther. But I don't have any money and I'd have to go to town and live there during the school year."

"I see," said James. You're certainly smart enough. What would you do once you graduated from there?"

"I was thinking I might like to go doctoring."

"I see," said James again.

"It's probably just a silly notion," said Roddy. He scooped up the last of his potatoes and gravy with his spoon.

"We'll talk about this again," said Beth. "It's really not a silly notion."

§

After chores were done and the lesson was read and a bedtime snack was consumed, Roddy and Maggie climbed the steep stairs to the sleeping loft.

"I'd like to have a proper set of stairs to the upstairs," said Beth. "I was thinking that the kitchen really needs to be bigger, and we could put new stairs in if we were to enlarge that end of the house. One of these years, we're not going to be able to climb those old loft stairs, and we'll be needing to sleep on this floor. We should make provisions now for our old age."

James chuckled. "You are thinking ahead." He sat contemplating what Beth had said then nodded. "Of course, you're right. It won't hurt to enlarge the kitchen and add a bedroom at the end. The house has never been changed since my grandfather built it when he came from Skye."

He sat silently for a few more minutes. Then carefully listening for the sounds of sleep from upstairs. "What d'you think about Roddy wanting to go on to junior college?"

Beth smiled and set down her knitting. "Who'd have thought when he came here?"

James nodded. "He's certainly smart enough." He rocked by the fire for a moment or two. We'll have to save our money for the next year and hope it's enough. It's not just the education and books, he'd have to have living expenses too."

Beth nodded and took up her knitting again.

"I know. I've been thinking about that lately, and I've been saving my egg money for the last year. I have quite a little bit put aside, and we can keep adding to it as we go."

James looked across at Beth. "You're a wonder! How'd you know?"

"Something I heard him say one day last year made me think that he might want to. I don't remember what it was. Just a word or two, but when I asked him, he dismissed it and deflected. You know how he can be."

"I guess he wasn't ready to talk about it. I know he didn't really want to talk about it this evening either. By the way, did you hear that Samuel and your brothers are going west for the harvest?"

Beth looked up from her task. "No! Where'd you hear that?"

"I ran into brother Robert this morning, and he told me. He heard it at the store last Saturday, but I haven't seen him to talk to since then. I ran into him on my way to the church meeting this afternoon."

"Well. Well." Beth felt her heart lift. "It's good riddance to them, then. Perhaps they'll stay there. Who's staying behind?"

"Robert said Ian decided not to go. He's been courting the widow Lizzie's daughter and doesn't want to leave her."

"Humph," said Beth. "It's probably the other

way around. She won't have wanted him to leave. Not that I wish her ill, but at least she's getting the best of the lot. She hasn't had any prospects, and she is getting on."

The boys left on the harvest train the next week and as predicted, they didn't return. It was rumoured that they pooled their money and bought acreage in Alberta, planning to run beef cattle.

Beth's relief was reflected in her posture and in her demeanour. She laughed more often and seemed more relaxed. James took note and breathed a sigh of relief. But the shadow of her crime was always in the back of her eyes. Sometimes, when she was alone, the enormity of her deed lay on her heart as heavily as ever it had, the memory of that terrible day as fresh as yesterday. And with Maggie and Roddy both in school, she was much alone. Laura Jean slept a lot, and James was making the farm snug for winter. The crops were harvested and stored in the barns with the reciprocal help from neighbours which meant that James was often away all day. Beth did her share for the women. She packed up Laura Jean in the wheelbarrow and surrounded her with loaves of warm bread and other baked goods and trundled them off to whoever had the crew in that day. The men were well fed, and the old women got lots of baby time with Laura Jean. She hardly ever slept outside of someone's arms. It was a time of great community.

In October, Beth realized that her time of month had been absent for several months. Perhaps I've gone through the change, she thought. It's a little sad to think of, but that's the way of it for all of us. She dismissed the thought from her mind. In December, she felt an odd, familiar touching in her belly and realized that her dresses had been getting tighter over the fall. Hope flared in her heart. Maybe, just maybe, she thought. The touching came again a few days later. She sat and reflected on the possibility. In the following weeks, she became very sure.

"James, what would you say if I told you that I think I'm expecting another baby?"

James glanced in the direction of the loft but all was quiet in sleep. "Are you sure?"

Beth nodded. "I haven't had my monthlies since August or September, and these last few days I've been feeling a little movement. Not much and it seems earlier than with Laura Jean, but it wasn't just dyspepsia."

James rose and came to Beth. He raised her from her chair and held her close. "I will welcome another child. I am, indeed, a fortunate man."

§

Over the winter, Beth grew round and heavy with child. Her heart was peaceful during this time and although she rarely thought actively about her father or her brothers, her secret still lurked in the background of her mind. I'm glad the boys stayed out west, she thought. It is such a relief to not have to be so watchful of me and the children. She sat in the rocker and observed them bent over their slates, Roddy because he had to, and Maggie because she wanted to copy Roddy and be like the big children. Her "homework" was just practising her letters and numbers over and over, and when she learned to spell simple words, they were added to the self-imposed activity. In late spring, Beth delivered another girl much to the delight of the others. Together they named her Elizabeth Anne.

In a quiet moment when the children had gone up to bed Beth asked: "Are you disappointed she's not a boy?"

James looked at her sharply. "Of course, not. Where in the world would you get such an idea?"

"I thought that men liked boys to carry on the family name. One of the ladies said the other day that we should have had a son for that reason."

"Och, old women! They create more trouble

with their nattering. A boy would have been fine, but my womenfolk are special. She'll grow up just like you, and with Laura Jean and you too, I will be surrounded in my old age."

The summer passed quickly. Roddy worked with James and when time permitted, for the other farmers around the community. He saved whatever coins they were able to give him for his work. The babies thrived. Laura Jean teethed and began to walk. Beth Anne was content to spend her time growing and watching alertly to all that went on around her. She was a placid infant and only cried when she was in real distress, hungry, wet or cold. Beth made Roddy a new suit of clothes for when he went to college. She secretly shed tears if she thought of how much she would miss him. She tried not to think too hard about the fast approaching day.

The evening before his departure, they sat together on the red sandstone stoop in the rays of the setting sun.

"I'll miss you," said Beth. She swallowed hard against the threatening tears. "You're my only son."

"Even though I'm not really yours?" asked Roddy.

Beth nodded. "You're mine in all the ways that count. I cannot imagine life without you. You were ours almost as soon as you stepped over the threshold."

Roddy threw his now manly arms around Beth and gave her one of his sloppy kisses on her cheek. "I'm glad I stole your cake that day."

"Are you nervous about going away from us?"

Roddy considered the question for a moment. "Not nervous as in scared, just excited to be learning some more, and I expect I'll be lonesome for you and Poppa if I think too hard about it. I'll miss the girls too. That Maggie is a smart little thing. She has a lot of ideas and deep thoughts."

Beth nodded. "I hope when the time comes she decides to go on too. It'd be a shame if she thought she had to stop at this school."

"It's harder for girls," said Roddy. "The jobs are all for men."

Beth sighed. "I know. It's a terrible thing to waste the minds and abilities of half the population."

Roddy was silent for a long time then. He stared out at the glory of the sunset as it faded into starry darkness. Then, "Beth? You know that I know what happened to your Pa."

Beth startled. "You do? How do you know that?"

Roddy shrugged. "I figured it out. You were being extremely generous with the fruitcake that day and with Poppa's rum. I knew where the rat poison was because I saw Poppa put it up there. And then a few days after your Pa's visit, it was gone and I knew that Poppa hadn't used it in the barn. Then we got news of his drowning. So I just figured it out." Roddy was silent for another moment. "Served him right!"

Beth was speechless. Then she thought of her daughters, and a great feeling of relief and healing washed over her. "It did serve him right."

Learn more about Margaret Westlie, her life
and her books, at:

www.margaretwestlie.com